UNINTENDED TARGET

MACARTHUR FAMILY SERIES

Katie Reus

Copyright © 2021 by Katie Reus.

All rights reserved. Except as permitted under the U.S. Copyright Act of 1976, no part of this publication may be reproduced, distributed, or transmitted in any form or by any means, or stored in a database or retrieval system, without the prior written permission of the author. Thank you for buying an authorized version of this book and complying with copyright laws. You're supporting writers and encouraging creativity.

Cover art: Jaycee of Sweet 'N Spicy Designs
Editor: Julia Ganis
Author website: https://www.katiereus.com

Publisher's Note: This is a work of fiction. Names, characters, places, and incidents are either the products of the author's imagination or used fictitiously, and any resemblance to actual persons, living or dead, or business establishments, organizations or locales is completely coincidental.

Unintended Target/Katie Reus. -- 1st ed.
KR Press, LLC

ISBN 13: 9781635561548

eISBN: 9781635561531

For all the great teachers who actively encourage creativity. You're helping to shape the world into a better place.

Praise for the novels of Katie Reus

"...a wild hot ride for readers. The story grabs you and doesn't let go."
—*New York Times* bestselling author, Cynthia Eden

"Has all the right ingredients: a hot couple, evil villains, and a killer action-filled plot. . . . [The] Moon Shifter series is what I call Grade-A entertainment!" —Joyfully Reviewed

"I could not put this book down. . . . Let me be clear that I am not saying that this was a good book *for* a paranormal genre; it was an excellent romance read, *period.*" —All About Romance

"Reus strikes just the right balance of steamy sexual tension and nail-biting action....This romantic thriller reliably hits every note that fans of the genre will expect." —*Publishers Weekly*

"Prepare yourself for the start of a great new series! . . . I'm excited about reading more about this great group of characters."
—Fresh Fiction

"Wow! This powerful, passionate hero sizzles with sheer deliciousness. I loved every sexy twist of this fun & exhilarating tale. Katie Reus delivers!" —Carolyn Crane, RITA award winning author

"A sexy, well-crafted paranormal romance that succeeds with smart characters and creative world building." —Kirkus Reviews

"*Mating Instinct*'s romance is taut and passionate . . . Katie Reus's newest installment in her Moon Shifter series will leave readers breathless!"
—Stephanie Tyler, *New York Times* bestselling author

"You'll fall in love with Katie's heroes."
—*New York Times* bestselling author, Kaylea Cross

"Both romantic and suspenseful, a fast-paced sexy book full of high stakes action." —Heroes and Heartbreakers

"Katie Reus pulls the reader into a story line of second chances, betrayal, and the truth about forgotten lives and hidden pasts."
—The Reading Café

"Nonstop action, a solid plot, good pacing, and riveting suspense."
—RT Book Reviews

"Exciting in more ways than one, well-paced and smoothly written, I'd recommend *A Covert Affair* to any romantic suspense reader."
—Harlequin Junkie

"Sexy military romantic suspense." —USA Today

"Enough sexual tension to set the pages on fire."
—*New York Times* bestselling author, Alexandra Ivy

"*Avenger's Heat* hits the ground running...This is a story of strength, of partnership and healing, and it does it brilliantly."
—Vampire Book Club

"*Mating Instinct* was a great read with complex characters, serious political issues and a world I am looking forward to coming back to."
—All Things Urban Fantasy

CHAPTER ONE

Patience Carras stared at her cell phone for a long moment, deciding if she should answer. She loved her mom, but right now Patience was stretched out on a lounge chair by her pool, margarita in hand.

She just wanted to relax, maybe get a slight buzz and a tan.

It had been a long year and school had just let out yesterday, so yes, she was day drinking and enjoying her Saturday with booze and sun. She would probably do the exact same thing tomorrow as well. But if she didn't answer, her mom would just call back in ten minutes. And then she might show up.

Sighing, she slipped in her Bluetooth so she could be hands-free and still drink her margarita while talking. "Hey, Mom."

"Hey, sweetheart. How's the first day of freedom?" she asked, laughing.

Patience snorted even though she truly missed her kids already. She said it every year but she'd had a great group of kids this year. To be honest, she preferred kids to adults. They told the truth, didn't have any malicious intentions for the most part, and they said the funniest things. All that other bad crap was taught to them by their parents or the world in general. But until that happened, they were wonderful, honest little humans. "I'm currently laying out by my pool, and yes, I have on SPF 75 before you ask."

Her mom snickered lightly. "Good. So, ah... What are your plans for the summer?"

Something about her mom's tone pinged on Patience's radar. "I've got a few trips planned with friends and a whole lot of relaxing. Why?" She took a sip of her drink and smiled at the sweet-tart taste.

"Well, I have a tiny favor to ask."

Oh no. Her mom's favors were never small.

"Just hear me out," she continued when Patience didn't respond. "You know the Robinsons."

Patience winced at the name. Yeah, she knew them. Vanessa and Josh Robinson had recently died in a freak helicopter crash. "How's Trevor doing anyway?" she asked.

Trevor was Josh's older brother and a few years older than her. He ran some sort of tech empire and had become a single dad overnight when he'd become his recently orphaned young nephew's guardian. Oliver would be nine or ten months old now.

"According to his mom, not great. You know Flora and I are on a couple charity boards together. The other day she told me that his last nanny quit on him. Again. Apparently he's gone through five in the last few months."

Nooooo. Patience knew exactly where this was going now. Before she'd become a teacher, she had been a nanny throughout college. "That's a ridiculously high turnover. Especially for someone like Trevor. Unless you're leaving out a key point to this." Also, babies were pretty easy because they weren't getting into anything yet. They needed a lot of attention but they also slept a lot at that stage. It was very Groundhog Day type of stuff: eat, sleep, poop, repeat.

"He doesn't understand what's going on either because the pay is above average, he's been using a reputable agency, and the schedule isn't excessive."

"I'm sorry to hear that he's struggling." And she truly was. She didn't know Trevor well but she knew his mom and adored her. And losing his brother and becoming an overnight parent had to be tough.

"Well?"

"Well what?"

"Are you going to make me say it?" her mom asked.

"If you're asking me to nanny, I don't do that anymore. I have a full-time job." One she loved.

"He's desperate. And he would pay you double his normal salary *just* for the summer while he tries to vet people and find someone who will actually stick around this time. Apparently one of the nannies kept hitting on him and that's why he ended up letting her go."

"I thought you said they all quit."

"*Most* of them quit. One he let go because she was more interested in him than doing her job."

The beginning of a tension headache started spreading against the back of her skull. "I'm not saying yes." So that was pretty much a lie. "I'll *talk* to him and see if we can work something out very temporarily. Just to reiterate, this is for the summer only." It didn't matter that her mom was currently saying *just for the summer*. She knew what would happen if Trevor didn't find someone by summer's end. And with her mom, she sometimes needed to make things crystal clear. "I'm not quitting my job."

"I knew you would help out!"

"I'm not starting today and I'm not starting tomorrow. In fact, I won't start until Wednesday at the earliest. I've got a lot of stuff to take care of. Just send me his phone number so I can talk to him."

"Check your email. I've already sent you all the details."

Of course she had. "So how's Dad?"

"Retirement definitely suits him. He's off on some fishing charter for the week."

"I'm sure you're suffering in his absence," she said laughingly. Her mom loved her dad but occasionally they needed a break from each other.

"We'll have fun once he gets back."

"I so don't need those details." Patience loved her parents, but that was just way too much. And now…she had a new schedule to figure out this summer.

* * *

"I can't believe you're working all summer," her friend Rebecca said as she sat on one of the benches a few feet down from the still busy nightclub.

Music trailed out every time the front door opened and a few people stumbled out. Clubs weren't really Patience's thing but her friends had wanted to go tonight. She preferred low-key bars and occasionally karaoke. Though she wasn't a night owl at all—she liked hiking, snorkeling and spending time at the beach. So when her friends had wanted to leave at midnight she was more than happy to head home.

"You mind getting me some tacos across the street? You know what I like," Rebecca said as she pulled a twenty from her purse. "Ooh, or maybe some grilled cheese sandwiches?"

Patience snorted. "Sure. How long do you think the others will be?"

"Well, I'm pretty sure Dustin is getting that bartender's phone number, so as long as it takes him. Then we can all ride-share together."

"Sounds good to me." She waved off Rebecca's money and stood.

As she hurried across the street toward the circle of food trucks, she cursed the heels pinching her feet. She wished she was at home in her pajamas, already sleeping. Or reading.

Since the taco truck had no line she stepped up to that one first and smiled at Marco—the owner of the food truck, who was working his way through college. She'd been down here enough on weekends hitting up the local farmers market that she knew him. "Two carne asada tacos, three chicken tacos, and three with shredded spicy beef, please."

He winked at her. "No problem."

"Make that five carne asadas." She turned at the sound of a deep male voice. The man slid a couple bills onto the countertop.

Raising her eyebrows, she looked up at the guy and blinked. *Oh my.* This guy took tall, dark and handsome to a new level. His brown hair was cropped close and he had a very nice bronze tan—as if he spent a lot of time outdoors. Or maybe he'd just spent a week on the water. His eyes were a dark forest green and he had a faint white mark on his cheek, from a long-healed scar. "You don't need to buy my tacos."

"I know. I just felt like doing something nice."

"I'm not giving you my phone number."

"Pretty sure I didn't ask." His oh-so-sexy mouth quirked upward slightly, revealing a dimple as he watched her with amusement.

She laughed lightly. "Okay. Just making sure you don't think that buying me tacos means you're getting anything. Also, thank you. That's very nice."

He lifted a shoulder. "No problem." Then he glanced away, as if looking for someone.

"Were you at the club across the street?" she asked, even though he wasn't exactly dressed for it. The club wasn't fancy but he had on jeans, a plain T-shirt and boots.

He snorted softly. "No."

"So what are you doing down here at this hour?" She wasn't sure why she was being so chatty. She'd like to blame it on having too many drinks, but she'd only had one before switching to water. This guy was just sexy as hell and she was curious about him.

He grinned as he looked down at her, and damn, those eyes were captivating. "I have no idea."

"You have no idea why you're downtown?"

The man who owned the taco truck handed them two bags.

"Keep the change," Mr. Sexy said.

Marco smiled at the two of them and handed over another small bag. "Thanks. Here's some extra guacamole."

Mr. Sexy handed her the guac bag and his sexiness meter went up even higher. "My sister asked me to meet her down here and I don't know why," he said, answering her earlier question. "I think she's screwing with me."

"Is that something she normally does?" If Patience didn't love her friends so much—both of whom were now waiting across the street for her—she would think about eating all these tacos by herself.

Instead of answering, he said, "Are you good, or do you want me to call you a ride or anything?" His voice was slightly distracted as he scanned a group of guys across the street who looked like they were definitely up to no good. They were eyeing a woman walking alone and starting to follow her.

Patience started to step forward, to do something, though she wasn't sure what, when a car pulled up and picked up said woman. "I'm fine, thank you."

He nodded and fell in step with her, but he kept a decent amount of distance between them, as if he didn't want to make her uncomfortable. Something she appreciated.

"So, if I asked for your phone number, would you give it to me?" His voice was deep, sexy and intoxicating. And the way he was watching her, with a hungry intensity she felt all the way to her toes...

She was tempted to say yes. Sooooo very tempted. "I want to, but I have no time to date this summer."

He laughed lightly, the sound rich and dark, like warm honey. "I appreciate the honesty. Enjoy the tacos and get home safe." Then he headed across the street in the other direction.

For some reason she was a little disappointed that he hadn't pushed for her phone number—even though she was simultaneously glad he hadn't. Pushy guys were dicks.

"Come on girl, I'm starving!" Rebecca's voice carried from across the street, pulling her back to reality.

Soon she'd be in her own bed, full from tacos and fast asleep. And she wouldn't be regretting not giving her number to Mr. Sexy.

Probably.

CHAPTER TWO

"You should have told me you were hiring someone," Brodie said to Trevor over the phone, annoyed he wasn't there in person.

"Pretty sure that's what I'm doing right now." His boss's tone was dry.

Brodie bit back his sigh of frustration. He worked for Trevor but the man also depended on Brodie to keep his life secure. "I mean so I could have done a background check. Clearly we've been dropping the ball somewhere and I don't like the thought of a stranger in your home." Especially after the last handful of nannies—hired through an incredibly reputable company—had quit with no notice. He'd tried talking to the company, but they'd absolutely refused to let him talk to any of the women because of confidentiality. Which he understood, but damn.

"She's not a stranger. Our families are friends and have been for ages. She has an impressive résumé and it's *only* for the summer until I can find a permanent replacement. This way I'm not stressing out and hiring someone who will just quit again in a week's time." His tone was even. "And I don't get it either. Oliver is so easygoing and adorable."

Brodie nodded even though Trevor couldn't see him. He was currently at an airport, waiting for his connecting flight, so he tuned out all the background noise. "We're never using that agency again, but I've narrowed down a couple that come highly recommended."

"Good. Until then, she starts today. She nannied in college and now she's a kindergarten teacher. Once you get back, you can see for yourself that she's great."

He'd definitely be checking her out. "How can you know she's great? She hasn't even started yet." And the fact that someone Brodie knew nothing about was in Trevor's home was making the back of Brodie's neck itch. He didn't like this at all even if she was a family friend.

"I'm not having this conversation."

"At least send me her information so I can do a basic run."

"No. You need to be focusing on what you're doing right now for *me*. Not hacking her life."

He was on a job for Trevor now researching a potential new location for one of his businesses in a fairly remote area. Trevor wanted eyes on the ground and a personal report from Brodie because he trusted him. "You won't even give me her name?"

"Nope."

Brodie took a deep breath. "Is she more than a friend or something?" he finally asked. He couldn't imagine Trevor hiring someone he was involved with, but he needed to check. Trevor dated about as much as him—pretty much never at this point. Though he'd hoped to break his no-dating streak with the sexy brunette from the other night. The woman with the bright Mediterranean eyes and curvy hips he easily imagined holding on to as he tugged her close.

Trevor let out a startled burst of laughter. "My God, no. Just no. She's too young for me and just...no."

At least that was something. Romance and business did not mix. "All right, then. I'll see you Friday."

"Safe travels."

Brodie shoved his phone in his pocket and pushed his annoyance back. They had a good security team at Trevor's house. Everyone was vetted, except for whoever this mystery woman was. Trevor wouldn't even give her name because he was right, Brodie would have dug deep.

He texted the man he'd left in charge, telling him to keep an eye on the new nanny. Then he asked what her name was.

He glared at his phone when Rick texted him back, *Will do. Also I've been instructed not to tell you her name. Sorry, boss.*

Brodie snorted, his mouth curving up. Trevor was thorough, he would give him that.

* * *

Patience stepped into Trevor's home office, glancing around at all the glass and sharp edges. He was seriously going to need to babyproof this space.

"What's that look?" he asked as he motioned for her to sit down in the black leather chair. He'd discarded his tie, and his jacket was tossed on the back of his chair, but he was still in slacks, a button-down shirt, and was wearing a watch she was pretty certain cost more than she made in a year as a teacher.

He really was observant. "I was just thinking you might want to babyproof in here."

He laughed lightly as he sat across from her, his dark brown eyes softening slightly. She'd interacted with him a few times over the years but he was a decade older and she didn't know him that well. But she'd always thought he was polished in that GQ sort of way. Looking at him right now, however, the man was clearly exhausted. His sandy blond hair was slightly mussed—and not in an "on purpose" type of way. He looked as if he'd been running his hands through it in agitation. "It's on my to-do list, I promise."

"So how are you doing? Seriously?" The guy had lost so much and gone from uncle to dad overnight. That was a whole lot for anyone.

"I want to lie to you and tell you I'm fine, but really I'm exhausted. *Babies* are exhausting. I love Oliver so much and I'm honored that my brother thought enough of me to make me his guardian, but…I'm running on fumes."

She'd read some business articles on him in the past and he'd seemed almost aloof and cold in them, but now he just seemed like a real man—a very tired one at his wit's end. She nodded. "That's so normal. And I know I've said it before, but I'm really sorry about your brother and sister-in-law."

His jaw tensed slightly. "Thank you."

"So I know we went over everything on the phone, but I'm a big believer in open communication, so like I said, I'll work weekdays, have weekends off. And I'll stay on-site in the guesthouse during the week because you get up so dang early for work." It was a position she'd been in before with families.

Living on-site during the week made things easier for everyone, herself included. But there was a downside to it. She'd found that she had to draw very clear boundaries when she lived on-site. Some parents had been of the mind that because she was nearby, she was available 24/7. For the most part she'd been able to create boundaries early, but with some parents she'd had to find other employment because they simply wouldn't listen.

His mouth lifted up slightly. "All that still works. And I have a service that cleans the house and guesthouse once a week, so I'll make sure to get you their schedule. Also, I have a chef, so I don't expect you to do any cooking."

"Good, because I suck at it. And it's very unlikely I'll stay here on weekends, so if it makes it easier for your crew to clean then, that's fine with me. Also…I'll be available for evening emergencies obviously, but once I'm off the clock I'm usually going to turn my phone off." Technically she wouldn't, but she wanted it clear that she wouldn't be answering her phone for anything but emergencies.

He smiled again. "I get it. And I'm glad you're being clear with your boundaries. I wish everyone I worked with was this transparent. And I really appreciate you doing this. I know summer is the time when teachers need to recharge."

She gave him a real smile. "It's all good. So what type of sleep schedule do you have Oliver on?"

He blinked at her once. "Sleep schedule?"

Oh no. So he really didn't have anything figured out. "Okay, so he's not on a sleep schedule, but that's okay. Does he sleep through the night?"

"For the most part, yes. But lately he's been waking up crying about three a.m. He's teething."

"Oh, that's the worst."

"I've been using a cool teething ring, which seems to help."

"Perfect. I've got a couple other things to try too."

"Thank God," he breathed out. "I hate seeing him in pain."

"I know it's on my résumé, but I'm CPR certified and if you're comfortable I'd love to take him in the pool occasionally—in the early mornings or late afternoons, with sunscreen and in a floatie I'll be holding the entire time," she added. "It's been my experience that babies love water and I want to keep him stimulated as much as possible. It will help him sleep more soundly at night."

"That sounds great. My mom's taken him in a few times and he seems to love it."

For the next fifteen minutes they talked about anything she thought might be pertinent, before they both stood. "Now how about you show me that sweet baby?"

she said, smiling. Flora had shown her pictures and he was the cutest thing. All chubby cheeks and big blue eyes.

"Gladly. My mom's here with him. I think they're in the kitchen now."

"I'm going to need a map to get around this place," she said as they stepped out into the hallway, only partially joking.

He snorted softly. "Oh, and my head of security is out of town but you'll meet him next week. He'll likely go over some stuff with you about the grounds here but I can't think of anything pertinent you need to know for now."

"Sounds good." Even though she'd had much different plans for the summer, she was glad to be able to help Trevor out. And Oliver. Poor thing had lost his parents and then gone through a string of nannies. Plus she'd be able to sock away some extra money, which was always a good thing.

CHAPTER THREE

Patience knocked gently on Trevor's office door, hoping she wasn't interrupting him. He'd gotten home half an hour ago and she was about to "clock out" for the day.

"Come in," he called out.

She opened the door and jerked to a halt to see Mr. Too Sexy For His Own Good standing next to Trevor's desk. What was the man who'd bought her tacos doing here? In a dark suit with no tie, just a white button-down shirt, tailored slacks and oh my God, those dark green eyes, he looked delicious.

His eyes widened slightly as he caught her gaze, clearly as surprised as she was.

"Patience, this is Brodie MacArthur, my head of security. The one I told you about."

"Oh, nice to meet you." Trevor had told her that the man was supposed to be back last week, but he'd apparently been kept away because of some business thing.

Brodie nodded politely, a mask of sorts falling into place, his expression going neutral. He sure wasn't looking at her the way he had the other night. "Nice to meet you too."

It was so weird seeing him here, sort of out of context for her brain, but she moved past it and turned back to Trevor. "I was hoping I could talk to you for a few minutes? But I can come back if you guys are busy. I was just about to head to the guesthouse."

"It's fine. Brodie was just leaving."

Brodie looked as if he wanted to disagree but he simply nodded and stepped outside, shutting the door behind him.

"I hope I didn't interrupt anything."

"No worries, trust me. Is everything okay?"

"Yep, everything's great. I just wanted to remind you that tonight is the first night I'm headed back to the guest cottage." Since Oliver hadn't been on a sleep schedule, she'd worked through all of last week and the weekend and stayed in the room next to his to get him situated and on a schedule. Now he was sleeping through the night like a dream even with his teething.

"I know, I've got it on my calendar," he said, laughing.

She was so glad he seemed to be a man of his word about respecting boundaries. So far there were no red flags and this job was easy, relatively speaking. Oliver needed a ton of attention, but he was a baby and that was to be expected. "Great, then. And just an update... There are no issues, and I'm honestly surprised you had those nannies quit so quickly. It's kind of bizarre." The place was gorgeous, with an Olympic-size pool—which she'd been in with Oliver, who loved it—a gym she had access to, and Oliver was an easy baby. He just wanted love and attention.

He looked relieved. "I'm glad to hear you say that. I've been racking my brain trying to figure out what went wrong before."

"So have you found an agency you like yet and started looking for someone permanent?" The sooner he got someone, the better it would be for everyone, especially Oliver. The fewer disruptions to his life right now, the better. Babies were so resilient, but still, he would need time to adjust to someone new. And if possible, she wanted to help out with the transition.

"Brodie has started hunting pretty seriously. He wants to do more intense background checks to make sure we don't run into the same thing as before. Though to be honest there weren't any red flags with the other women, so…" He lifted a shoulder, looking more like the man she'd known for years—well rested and put together.

"Okay, then. I'll let myself out."

"Make sure you grab something from the kitchen. Antoine said he left a casserole in the fridge and I won't be able to eat it all. Anything in there is yours. And if you have any requests, let Antoine know as well."

She hadn't actually met his chef yet, she'd been so busy with Oliver. She had tasted some of his pecan sandies and they'd been incredible. Apparently he was some sought-after French chef. "That's great, thanks. Oh, I actually did want to ask about that. Is it okay if I bake occasionally for myself in the kitchen when I'm with Oliver? I'll use my own ingredients."

"Seriously, anything you want to do is fine—and use whatever's in the pantry. Look, I trust you. And I'm grateful that you took up this position so last-minute. Are you sure you don't want a permanent job?" he asked, half-jokingly.

"I'm sure. I love what I do." Even though Oliver was sweet enough to tempt her to stay on permanently under different circumstances.

"All right, then," he said, standing with her. "I'm going to go check on Oliver."

She handed him the monitor she'd been carrying around. He was currently playing with one of the security guys in the living room, which meant he was sitting there in his Melissa & Doug turtle ball pit and gumming one of the plastic balls as he babbled to himself. "He'll go to sleep in two hours if he sticks to his schedule."

"The bouncer was a good idea," he said as they stepped into the hallway.

"I used to nanny for a baby who would bounce himself to sleep, wake up, then start all over again. That kid is now six and killing it in gymnastics." She'd stayed in touch with some of the families she'd worked for—and had a couple of the kids in her classes.

He laughed lightly and nodded once at Brodie—who she was probably going to keep thinking of as Mr. Sexy—who was standing outside the office door. The man nodded at Trevor, who kept going.

Patience stopped in front of the broad-shouldered head of security, feeling all sorts of awkward. "Hey, it's kind of weird seeing you here." She immediately winced at herself. *Way to be Captain Obvious.*

He nodded a little stiffly. "It is. So you're friends with Trevor?"

She lifted a shoulder. "Ah, our families are friends. Our moms really. We were always friendly I guess, but he's older and we went to different schools so we never ran in the same circles." And while her parents had done well for themselves, Trevor was in a different league altogether because of his tech companies.

Brodie nodded once, watching her carefully.

She felt as if she was under a microscope and not in a good way. He definitely wasn't looking at her the way he had been the other night. No, then he'd been looking at her in the way a man looks at a woman he wants to get naked with.

She had this insane need to fill silences and she hated that about herself. But she couldn't stop herself from continuing to talk. "Did you ever find your sister that night?" she asked, because he said he'd been waiting for her.

He scowled and somehow it made him look even sexier. "No."

All right then, she'd made it worse. So this was just really super freaking awkward. "I'm going to grab some food and then head back to the guesthouse. Unless you need me for something?" She wasn't sure why he was hanging out here. Had he been waiting to talk to her? If so, why wasn't he saying anything?

"Nope. I assume Trevor went over everything with you."

She shrugged. She wasn't sure if he was talking about baby stuff, but she definitely had all that under control. "Yep. I'm good."

"Okay. Let me know if you need anything."

As she headed down the hallway, she could feel his eyes on her. And for some reason she didn't think he was checking out her ass as she walked away. Which was pretty disappointing.

CHAPTER FOUR

Patience slowed her jog as she reached the gate at Flora's house and pressed the buzzer. The gate rolled open immediately and she pushed the stroller up the driveway, enjoying the cloudless day. She'd been taking Oliver out for strolls around the property and swimming with him in the pool, but today she'd decided to jog over to Trevor's mom's place for a change of scenery.

Before she'd even reached the middle of the circular driveway, Flora threw open one of the wide arched doors and strode out toward them. Her spiral-curly hair had gone gray years ago and she'd embraced it, making it work for her. She had on flowing linen pants and a matching linen shirt, both cream-colored. Wearing a single-strand diamond necklace and what were most definitely real diamonds in her ears, she was graceful and put together as always.

"You're an angel, bringing me this sweet baby today. It's only been three days and I already miss him." Patience laughed as Flora expertly unstrapped him and took him out of the stroller. He squealed in delight as she kissed his cheeks and then cuddled him close. "Want to come in for some tea?"

"Do you have coffee?" she asked as she maneuvered the stroller up the few steps.

"I sure do. I would offer you a mimosa but—"

"Ha, ha. I'm not drinking while on the clock."

"Well I'm certainly glad to hear that you're not drinking while watching my grandson." She winked at her as she shut and locked the door behind them. "So why don't you tell me all about Trevor and what I've missed with Oliver the last couple days while you make some coffee. Just make yourself at home," Flora said as they stepped into the huge kitchen.

With dark gray cabinets, a sparkling white tile backsplash, huge wood beams running across the ceiling, hanging pendant lights, double ovens, an industrial-sized refrigerator—and a full-size wine refrigerator—this place was a show kitchen for sure.

Flora sat at the oversized center island and gently set Oliver on the gray-and-white veined countertop, holding on to him tight as he bounced in place.

"Well I finally got him on a sleep schedule," Patience said as she headed for the thankfully easy to operate Keurig coffee machine. "I worked through last weekend to make sure it would stick, and according to Trevor he slept through the night for him as well. And you know that he needs to start looking harder for nannies. Especially if you want to get a good one. He's only got a couple months to go." Less than, actually, since summer break was barely two months as it was. She put a mug underneath the one-cup brewer and turned to face Flora, who was cooing at Oliver.

"I don't want to know about all that, silly girl. I want to know about *Trevor*. How is he doing? Is he coming home at a good time? Is he eating properly? Is he dating? If so, what are his dates like?"

She stared, surprised at Flora, who was never this nosy. At least not around Patience. "No way. That's not what this visit is about. I'm not your little spy."

Flora grinned, clearly not put off. "Well I had to try, didn't I? Your mom said you wouldn't tell me anything and it looks as if she was right. And now I owe her ten dollars."

Patience laughed as she pulled the full mug out from under the brewer. "Do you have creamer or sugar?"

"Both. Creamer's in the fridge and sugar is in that canister." She nodded at a plain white one next to the coffee maker before lifting up Oliver's T-shirt and blowing a raspberry on his tummy.

He giggled maniacally and patted her face.

"I just worry about him. He works so much," she said as she sat back up and nestled Oliver in her lap. "He took the loss of his brother harder than I know he's letting on."

Patience simply nodded and sat across from Flora, listening as the other woman talked. They chatted and played with Oliver for an hour and a half before Oliver started getting cranky.

"I think I need to get him back home. It's almost time for his nap and it will be good to keep naptime in the same location, at least for now." The consistency was good when she could swing it.

"Of course. I might take him a couple days next week, but I'll let you know. I'm definitely scooping him up this weekend."

"Whatever works for you. I really am enjoying taking care of him." Sure, she missed what could've been an amazing summer, but Oliver was such a sweet little baby. Being around him made her realize how much she wanted one of her own. Not now or anything, but eventually. She just needed to meet the right person before she could consider that. For some strange reason the image of tall, dark and sexy Brodie MacArthur popped into her head. Which was…beyond ridiculous. The man didn't even seem to like her now. He watched her almost warily, as if expecting her to steal the silver.

"I wish there had been a spark between you and Trevor. Then I would've gotten to call you my daughter-in-law."

She blinked in surprise as they reached the foyer. Oliver patted her face gently and made little babbling sounds as he tried to imitate their words. "That's probably the sweetest thing you've ever said to me."

"Well it's true. Then your mom and I would be related. I think of her as a sister anyway, but still, it would have been nice."

She shifted Oliver slightly on her hip and he curled up against her, all soft squishiness. "I know she thinks very highly of you. She calls you the sister of her heart."

"All right, that's enough of this. I don't want to get all teary-eyed and ruin my mascara," she said as they stepped out into the bright sunlight. "I'm surprised that

Brodie allowed you to come down here without a guard." She frowned as she glanced down the driveway. "Unless they're just really good at blending in?"

Patience frowned even as her heart rate kicked up the tiniest notch at the mention of Brodie. "Allowed me?"

"Oh yeah. He's crazy about Trevor's security. And with good reason. In fact..." She pulled out her cell phone and texted somebody.

Unease stirred in her stomach. "Is there something I should know about?" Trevor had seemed pretty relaxed about everything, and she and Brodie hadn't talked much since that awkward conversation. He was kind of standoffish—and unfortunately sexy as hell so she couldn't remain completely oblivious to him. The man was impossible to ignore.

"Maybe. Trevor has had a few scares in the last couple years. It's all work stuff, not personal. But still, it's why Brodie ramped up security at Trevor's home. He doesn't go anywhere but the office and home—or work travel. He bought the giant monstrosity with all that land so he'd have space and privacy. Also...Brodie is sending someone to pick you up," she said as she looked at her phone.

She raised her eyebrows. "Is that really necessary?" Her stomach tightened that they needed to worry about security like that, and she had been clueless until now. She would have been more careful, but no one had said anything when she'd left this morning. Of course...she hadn't checked in or anything, she'd just left.

"I'll let you figure that out with Trevor or Brodie. I'm pretty sure they're going to want you to have a guard on you at all times if you're out with Oliver."

Well, if that was the deal while she was working for Trevor, then she'd just put up with it. She'd worked for wealthy clients before and a few of them had their own in-house security. Though no one had as much as Trevor. "So what do you think of Brodie?" she asked, unable to help herself. She tried to keep her voice oh so casual.

Oliver mimicked her then and tried to say Brodie, but it came out in baby-babble.

Flora's eyes narrowed ever so slightly before she took Oliver from her arms and put him in his carrier. "Is that interest I hear?"

"*No.* Mere curiosity. He's kind of intense." And soooo damn sexy. "And you'd better not say anything to my mom."

"I won't say anything if you tell me if Trevor has been taking care of himself."

"Fine. Yes, he comes home fairly early, from what I understand his schedule used to be, and he takes over with Oliver immediately. Sometimes he seems worried that he'll break him, but I've seen them together a couple times playing peekaboo in the kitchen and it's crazy cute. Oliver absolutely adores him. I'll take some pictures and send them to you."

Flora's expression softened at that. "Thank you. I'd love to have some of the two of them. You know, I was a little hurt that my son left Oliver to Trevor, but he knew what he was doing. I can see it now. My husband

and I enjoy being grandparents—which is a lot different than being parents."

"He's in good hands."

"Well, to answer your earlier question, Brodie MacArthur has been with Trevor for a decade now. He's good at what he does. I know his parents and like them. And as far as I know he is not a serial dater. Not... What is it that you kids say? He's not a manwhore."

Patience choked on air as Flora said the word *whore*, then she grinned. "Well I wasn't asking about that per se, but that's good to know."

She gave her a knowing look. "You were definitely asking."

Patience glanced over as the gate started to open. "Did you do that?"

Flora patted her pants pocket. "Remote control."

"Oh, right. Thank you for the coffee and company. I'll see you later."

"Sooner rather than later." Flora kissed her on the cheek and did the same to Oliver before waving at the SUV coming up the drive. Then she disappeared back inside.

Patience was surprised to find Brodie himself pulling up, aviator shades pushed onto his head as he stepped out of the driver's seat. And he looked...annoyed. Maybe even angry.

"Hey, you didn't have to come down here. It's just a short jog back," she said, smiling—and ignoring the stupid butterflies that took flight at just the sight of him.

His jaw tightened once, and oh—he was definitely angry.

"You're not supposed to leave the house without a guard." It was clear he was trying to remain polite, though his words were tight. She wondered if he was always this rigid and controlled.

She lifted the carrier out of the stroller and started securing it into the back seat. "I didn't realize. Trevor never said anything." Or if he had, she didn't remember. Crap, what if he had? No...she definitely would have remembered.

"Don't do it again," he gritted out.

Now she was starting to get annoyed. "I said okay. You don't need to tell me more than once." She wasn't a child and his anger was starting to irritate her. "If you're so worried, you could have just called me." She knew he had her number from Trevor.

"I did call you."

"Oh..." She winced. "I might've left my phone in the diaper bag."

"We were pretty damn close to calling the police."

She turned to stare at him as she shut the door on Oliver. "Seriously?"

He sighed, some of the steam leaving him but not all of it. "Yes. Trevor has had a few scares at work lately. We take his security and now Oliver's very seriously. I saw you on the security feed leaving of your own accord. I figured you'd gone to a local park so we've been out scouring. I didn't even think of Flora's place."

Okay, so now she felt bad that they'd been out looking for them. "Crap, I really am sorry. I would never do anything to put Oliver in danger."

"I know that. Get in," he said tiredly.

"Is there a serious threat? Like...should I be worried or taking precautions?" she asked as he slid into the driver's seat.

"No. There's nothing current right now. I was just...concerned."

That made her feel better at least. The drive back only took a few minutes, but they were ridiculously tense. She'd never felt so awkward in her life as she tried to think of something neutral to say. Something. Anything! But her tongue felt too big for her mouth and her brain had completely given up on her. *Ugh. Just great.* Being around him, when he clearly didn't like her, was messing with her head. She wasn't used to people not liking her.

"What are you doing now?" he asked when they finally got inside the house.

"Oliver's already dozing so I'm going to get him down in his crib and then grab a quick bite to eat." She'd had a lot of coffee over at Flora's but hadn't eaten anything of substance and she was regretting it now.

"When you're done will you meet me in my office?"

"Sure." She knew where his office was, right next to Trevor's. Trevor had pointed it out to her, but she'd never been in there.

Fifteen minutes later, she half knocked on the already open door. Her stomach tightened slightly—she'd apologized and she clearly wouldn't leave again without a guard for Oliver, but she wondered if there was more to this threat that she should know about? He'd said no, but...his expression was impossible to read.

"Everything good?" Brodie stood as she entered, and even though the office was normal-sized, he seemed to suck up all the space with his dark appeal. He pinned her in place with those dark green eyes and she cleared her throat.

"Yep. So what's up?" She still hadn't eaten and wanted to get this over with. Mainly because being around him short-circuited her brain a bit. And that was just plain embarrassing since he didn't feel the same.

She glanced around the office and noticed immediately how spartan it was. There were bookshelves filled with some books, but mainly notebooks filled with who knew what. The furniture was high-quality, and the huge window behind his desk had gorgeous damask drapes that she guaranteed he hadn't hung up—no, a decorator had most likely done that. Brodie MacArthur didn't seem like the kind of man to pay attention to decorations.

"Normally I do all the vetting for anyone Trevor hires. Here and anyone at his office. My company is in charge of doing security checks."

She simply nodded because she wasn't sure where this was going.

"I would've done yours as well but he assured me you were a family friend."

Um...okay. "What's this about?" Clearly he was leading up to something, but she had no idea what it could be. And she wasn't going to play some weird word games with him trying to figure it out. Especially not when she was moving into hangry territory.

"I called some of your former employers and talked to a Richard Miller."

Ice coated her veins at his words even as anger simultaneously spiked inside her, all sharp, angry talons. "And?" Oh, she *really* wanted to know where he was going with this.

"And it sounds as if you had some problems with him and his wife."

She laughed then, she couldn't help it. "I kind of want to let you talk just to see what stupid thing you're going to say, but I'm going to go ahead and stop you right there. Because I can imagine where this is going. Did you happen to talk to *Alice* Miller?"

He shifted slightly in his seat, his eyes narrowing. "I called her cell phone and left a message but haven't heard back."

"Well, way to do your due diligence, jackass," she snapped at him. *Maybe* she was overreacting but she didn't care. It wasn't like Oliver was around and could hear her. And Brodie wasn't her boss. So yeah, she was angry. For being treated as a suspect when she was a good person and doing Trevor a huge favor. "Richard Miller harassed me to the point where I was close to quitting. He finally took it too far and I had to press charges against him for physical assault—which was well on its way to being a sexual assault if I hadn't stopped him. His wife left him and has full custody of their children. There is a whooooole lot more to that story than his take. As far as I know, he's only allowed to have supervised visits—if that. *She* is my reference, not him. I don't even know if he's allowed to talk about me to anyone. I'm not sure of all the legalities, but the fact that he clearly lied to you and you just believed whatever crap he said..." She shoved up from her chair, her whole body a trembling mass of rage.

He stood with her. "Patience, I'm—"

"Don't say my name. This is bullshit. I'm working here as a favor. I had an amazing summer mapped out, but I changed my plans because of what happened to Trevor and his family. But I'm not going to put up with being around you for the next two months. So I'm officially giving my two weeks' notice now. I will help Trevor find someone, if you get that far in the interview process by two weeks, and that's it. In fact, now I have a pretty good idea why you've lost so many nannies!"

Without waiting for his response, she strode out of the room, unable to be in his presence for another second. She hadn't thought about Richard Miller in years and Brodie had just brought up one of the most traumatic memories of her life.

He called her name, but she kept going. If she looked at him again, she was afraid she might cry tears of rage. She wouldn't give that jackass the satisfaction of seeing her cry.

CHAPTER FIVE

Brodie stepped through the open doorway to Trevor's office to find his boss sitting behind his desk. Instead of his normal business suit and tie, Trevor had changed into jeans and a T-shirt. "Oliver asleep?"

Trevor nodded and leaned back in his chair, covering a yawn. "What are you still doing here? It's late. Oh hell, do we have another threat? This deal is going to kill me," he muttered, rubbing his hands over his face.

Brodie cleared his throat, for the first time in as long as he could remember feeling...not nervous, but he hated that he had to have this conversation. Because Brodie was the one who had screwed up.

Big time.

"I screwed up," he said bluntly. There was no sense in dragging this out. And Trevor was the kind of guy who appreciated when he got to the point.

Surprise flickered across Trevor's face as he shifted his laptop away slightly. "How?"

"With Patience."

Now he shut his laptop. *"How?"*

"I wanted to look into her a little more. Since we've had such bad luck with the last few nannies. I found something in her background and questioned her about it. What I found was... Well it doesn't matter. I screwed up. I didn't accuse her of anything but I might as well have." He'd been well on his way to until she'd called him out. "It was a dick move and I didn't handle things professionally—"

"Fix it," Trevor snapped as he stood. "Because if you tell me she's going to quit, I'm going to lose my mind. I'm working on a huge deal right now, and as you know, I'm not sleeping well. I love Oliver, but holy shit babies are exhausting. And I have *help*. Better than I imagined. I can't afford to lose her right now. Did she say she was going to quit?" he demanded.

Brodie cleared his throat. "Yes."

Trevor rubbed a hand over his tired face and looked over at the monitor when Oliver started fussing slightly in his sleep. "I don't care what you have to do, but fix this. Apologize, grovel, tell her I'll give her a raise, but make it right." Then he strode from the room, not waiting for a response.

Brodie winced, berating himself. He'd begun digging into Patience and he had truly screwed up this time in a way he'd never done before. Not with work-related stuff. He should have waited until he had a better picture of her, done more thorough research. Instead he'd jumped the gun and... *Damn it.* He wasn't going to wait until tomorrow to talk to her. He radioed his people and told the man patrolling near the guesthouse that he was headed that way.

It didn't take long to get to the guesthouse, which was on the other side of the expansive pool. He knocked on the navy blue door of the cottage and frowned when it opened slightly. "Patience?"

He hadn't heard a report that she'd left the grounds, but maybe she had. No, she wouldn't leave Trevor high and dry like that and he'd instructed his people to tell him about her comings and goings.

He stepped into the little cottage and called out again. "Patience?" In response he heard a slight groan.

Shutting the door behind him, he moved into action, all his training kicking in as he drew his weapon.

The groan was coming from her bedroom. No one should have been able to breach the security here. Her bedroom was clear, with the lamp on the side table turned on and the comforter slightly rumpled on one side. He twisted suddenly at another groan coming from the bathroom—and he jerked to a halt when he found her slumped over the toilet. Her long, dark hair was shoved behind her ears and her T-shirt and jeans were rumpled.

She blinked up at him, her bright Mediterranean blue eyes bleary. "What are you doing here?" she rasped out.

He'd already tucked his weapon away before he crouched down next to her. He held the back of his hand to her forehead. She was clammy, and didn't seem to have a hot temperature. "What's wrong? Do you have the flu?"

She shook her head and shifted positions, leaning back against the bathtub. "Food poisoning. I've had it before." She closed her eyes and leaned her head back as she took a few shallow breaths.

Well shit. "I'll be back." Moving quickly, he jumped to his feet.

He hurried to the kitchen, checked her cabinets and the pantry to see what she had—it wasn't much. Then he put some ice in a plastic sandwich baggie, grabbed a washcloth and a little garbage pail from the pantry and brought it to the side of the king-size bed before hurrying back into the bathroom.

She was clutching onto the countertop of the sink, struggling to her feet.

Brodie steadied her before scooping her into his arms. She was slender and soft against him, something he didn't want to be noticing.

She blinked at him, a frown pulling at her pretty mouth. Damn, her lips were full, something he didn't want to notice either. "What are you doing?"

"Helping you get to bed. Is that what you were trying to do?"

She groaned and laid her head against his shoulder as if unable to hold it up anymore. "Yeah. I need to be horizontal for a while."

Gently he carried her to the bedroom and stretched her out on her back.

She kept her eyes closed, and when he put the bag of ice on her forehead she breathed out a sigh of relief. "Feels good," she murmured. "I just want to sleep." Her voice was thready.

"You sure this is food poisoning?" She was so damn pale—her skin had a gray pallor instead of the light bronze tan and he didn't like it.

"Yeah," she mumbled. "Had this twice before. I've got…a sensitive stomach I guess."

"I've got a plastic garbage pail right next to you if you get sick and can't make it to the bathroom." Not that he planned to leave or anything. Now wasn't the time to apologize and beg her to stay, but he was sure as hell going to take care of her. He couldn't leave her when she was in this condition. He couldn't leave anyone like this.

Stepping out of the room, he radioed one of his guys, asking the man to head out to buy Pedialyte and crackers on the company card. Tomorrow morning, she would very likely want to try eating something, and saltine crackers were the way to go, in his experience. And Pedialyte was what his mom had always gotten him and his siblings when they'd been sick.

"And grab some of those fruit popsicle things." He figured they'd be good for her throat. Once he'd done that, he called Flora. He wanted to make sure Flora could watch Oliver the next day. She told him that of course she was more than happy to watch her grandson so that took care of that.

Then he called Trevor, who was concerned but also relieved that Brodie had already taken care of the childcare situation. Once he was done, he stepped back into the bedroom to find Patience exactly as he'd left her, her eyes barely open as she stared at him.

"You're still here?" she murmured, then winced and closed her eyes again.

"I'm not going anywhere. I called Trevor and he knows what's going on. Flora will be taking over for tomorrow at least. All you need to focus on is sleep and getting better."

"I don't want you to hear or see me throwing up," she muttered more to herself than him.

"It's not a big deal." It was just one of those life things. People got sick.

She made a sort of grumbling sound before she jerked upright and promptly threw up in the garbage pail next to the bed.

He moved quickly and sat next to her on the bed, holding her hair away from her face while he simultaneously rubbed her back in gentle circles with his other hand.

When she was done, he took the pail from her even though she tried to stop him. "I got this."

"Ugh," she mumbled before flopping back on the bed. It was clear she was too weak to argue as she put the ice on her forehead again.

Since she was too weak to argue, she definitely wasn't able to take care of herself. He hated seeing her like this and was surprised by the protectiveness that swelled up inside him, at the need to take care of her. It had nothing to do with wanting her to forgive him. He simply wanted to make sure she got better.

After he'd cleaned out the pail, he picked up a hair band from the countertop and stepped back into the bedroom. "You think you can sit up for a minute?" he asked.

She groaned but pushed up on shaking arms.

He set the pail down on the floor and sat next to her. "I'm going to braid your hair so it's out of your face." It was probably overly familiar since he didn't know her well—and he'd been a giant dick to her—but he wanted to help.

She made some sort of nonsensical sound, but didn't move away from him so he gathered her dark hair and braided it in the world's worst braid. It was all uneven with one side thicker than the other, but at least it was out of her face.

"Thank you," she mumbled, her eyes closed as she lay back down. "You can go now."

Yeah, he wasn't going anywhere. He moved to the armchair by the window and sat. He'd sleep here all night if needed.

CHAPTER SIX

Patience groaned as she sat up, glad that the nausea from last night and most of the early morning hours seemed to have subsided. Her stomach muscles were sore from getting sick so often and she felt disgusting.

She hurried to the bathroom and quickly stripped out of her clothes. A shower with her favorite mango-scented shampoo and coconut body wash made her feel a billion times better. Finally, brushing her teeth with a minty-fresh toothpaste made her feel human again. Instead of drying her hair, she rebraided it, mainly because she was too weak to attempt using a hair dryer for longer than a few seconds. Her entire body just felt wrung out and taking a shower had sapped most of her energy. She dressed in comfortable lounge pants and a pullover sweater that was one of her favorites because it had been washed so many times. It didn't matter that it was summer; she wasn't planning on stepping outside the cottage today and she had the air-conditioning on low.

When she stepped out of the bedroom into the kitchen, she was surprised to find sexy-as-hell Brodie MacArthur leaning against the countertop, looking at something on his phone. He wore dark slacks and a button-down shirt—sans jacket and tie—his jaw tight as he read with complete concentration.

But the moment he noticed her, he immediately tucked his cell phone away and straightened. His clothing was the same, so he must have stayed the whole night. She...didn't understand why he was still here.

"Hey, how are you feeling?" The deep rumble of his voice rolled through her and, for some reason, soothed her.

The cottage wasn't very big, with the kitchen extending into the little living room. A countertop and high-top stools were the only separation so she went to sit at the marble countertop as she answered him. "Decent. Not like I'm going to throw up again anyway."

"I've got chicken soup, Pedialyte, which I recommend to help you rehydrate, even if it is tart, and saltines."

"Saltines are good for now. And yeah, Pedialyte is..." Well, it was gross. She knew it would be good for rehydrating but the thought of actually drinking it made her gag reflex trigger. *Ugh.* "Do you have any Propel? Or even tap water is good."

"I had one of my guys get a little of everything, including Propel." He opened the refrigerator and grabbed one of the bottles.

"Not that I'm not grateful you stayed—because I am. Very much so. Thank you for staying last night and for getting me food and drinks." And for braiding her hair, something she was still in a bit of shock over. "But what are you still doing here?" she asked as he opened the bottle and slid it across the countertop to her. She was careful not to let their fingers brush—for her own sanity. She was way too attracted to this man and he'd seen her throw up multiple times. Not only that, he'd cleaned out her throw-up bucket. Just...awesome. Not to mention he'd been a giant jerk to her before all her sickness.

"Originally I came to apologize and then I couldn't leave when I saw how sick you were." The worry in his eyes was the kind you couldn't fake. Or if he was faking, he was a damn good actor.

And it completely thawed her out toward him. Yeah she'd been pretty angry at him before, but after she'd had time to settle down, she'd decided not to quit. Even if he had acted like a giant dick, she wasn't going to leave Trevor and Oliver in the lurch. They'd already lost too much. But Brodie had been taking care of her for almost...fifteen hours. It was kind of hard to stay mad at someone who'd done that.

"Look, I'm really sorry we got off on the wrong foot," he said.

"We?" She lifted an eyebrow before bringing the bottle to her lips. The cool liquid rolled down her throat, soothing every part of her.

He snorted, his mouth curving up in a way that changed his entire countenance, making him look almost approachable. "Okay *me*. I'm sorry for, well, everything. I'm normally much better at vetting people and I jumped the gun because I didn't want Trevor to lose someone else again."

"Trevor's mom told me what happened with some of his former employees."

Brodie shook his head in frustration. "We vetted everyone thoroughly. So I don't understand what happened. I was just feeling protective of Trevor and Oliver and I completely screwed up. I'm sorry I brought up something that's clearly a painful part of your past, and that I was ready to believe the worst of you. There's no excuse for my behavior."

At least he wasn't making justifications, he was owning his bad actions. She appreciated that. "Apology accepted. And thank you for taking care of me last night. You went above and beyond what I would expect from a virtual stranger. You didn't have to stay and I appreciate it." Even if she did hate that he'd seen her throwing up. *Gah.*

He lifted a shoulder as if it was no big deal.

"Look, I'm not going to quit," she continued. "I said that in the heat of the moment because I was pretty mad at you. Rightfully so. But I'm not going to leave Trevor high and dry like that. I'll stick around until he finds someone or until the end of the summer. Whichever one comes first."

He nodded once, relief flickering in his dark green eyes. "Thank you."

When he didn't make a move to leave, she cleared her throat. "I promise I'm okay now. You don't need to stick around." She felt kind of weird with him in her personal space now that she was thinking clearly. He was so big and seemed to sort of take up the whole room with his presence.

He frowned at her. "Do you feel up to trying some chicken soup with your saltines?" he asked instead of responding.

Since she didn't feel like making soup for herself, she nodded. "Actually that sounds good. Just a little bit anyway," she said before nibbling on another cracker.

He dumped the contents of the soup into a pan and put it on the stovetop before turning it to simmer.

"You can just nuke it if you want." She so didn't care how it was prepared.

"It'll taste better this way."

She shrugged, but smiled as she eyed his backside. It felt surreal, having this big, strong, way too sexy man taking care of her. She should probably be embarrassed that he'd seen her throw up—and she kind of was—but he hadn't made her feel weird about anything. He'd simply stepped up and helped out. Even if it had been from guilt, he'd still been there. That mattered.

"Flora said you've been with Trevor for close to a decade," she said, wanting to make conversation—and hopefully learn more about him. She couldn't even try to squash her curiosity about him.

"Yep. He was my first client. And he's still my number one priority."

She took another sip of the Propel and wondered what kind of boyfriend Brodie would be—how he would prioritize a woman. After seeing him in action last night she imagined he'd probably be pretty incredible stepping up when needed. She shelved those thoughts, however, because it didn't matter. It wasn't like there was ever going to be anything between them. Sure, there had been a little spark between them at the food truck, but that felt like a decade ago instead of weeks.

As she drank more water, she immediately felt better and took a few more huge gulps. She was definitely going to need to rest until tomorrow morning to recover. Handling a baby in this condition wouldn't be smart. "Is Trevor really going to be okay without me? I know he's working on some big project."

"Flora has taken over everything. She said to take as long as you need to rest. What did you eat, by the way? I'd like to narrow it down to make sure no one else gets sick."

"I didn't eat much yesterday. I had cereal before I got Oliver up. Coffee, of course, and then I grabbed a few cookies from the main kitchen before coming back here." They'd been fresh, warm and incredible. Now she thought they'd probably gotten her sick. *Ugh.* Probably gotten cross-contaminated with something.

He nodded thoughtfully as if he was making a mental note of everything. "I'm sorry you got sick."

"Yeah me too. I've had food poisoning before and as you saw, it's not a fun experience. Ah…I'm also sorry you had to *see* me sick," she said because she wanted to get it out there.

He shrugged one of his big shoulders as if it was absolutely no big deal. "You don't have anything to be sorry for."

"Well thank you anyway. Listen, I really am okay. I appreciate you making the soup for me. After I eat, I'm probably going to lie down for a while and just rest. But I don't feel sick anymore. Just weak." As if she'd spent the day on a deep-sea diving boat and gotten knocked around by wave after wave.

He nodded, but paused as if he didn't want to leave. Then he set his business card down on the countertop. "I wrote my cell number on the back. Just call if you need anything."

"I will. And thank you."

His sexy lips pursed once. "You don't need to thank me again. I just did what anyone would have—and I should apologize again."

She laughed lightly because not everyone would have stepped up like that. "Okay so how about you don't apologize again and I won't thank you again and we'll call it even?"

His lips curved up and oh, damn, maybe it was because she was already feeling so weak, but she felt that smile in places she had no business feeling it. He was...sexy. There really was no other word for it. And that dimple was simply adorable.

His smile had just a hint of wicked, and while he wasn't handsome in that classical sense, he had a sort of rough-and-tumble air about him. As if he knew how to handle himself—which made sense given his profession. She couldn't help but wonder if he'd be able to handle himself in the bedroom.

When he finally left, she felt the strangest sense of loss. All she wanted to do was sleep right now, but...she still liked being around Brodie. And she wanted to get to know him more. A lot more.

Considering they worked with each other—sort of—that seemed like a bad idea.

CHAPTER SEVEN

Brodie found Trevor in the kitchen, sitting at the center island in front of a chicken burrito bowl and a glass of red wine.

"How is she?" Trevor asked, setting his tablet down. He was working with various local government entities around the state on growing mini-forests in unused areas, schoolyards, smaller downtown areas where space would allow, and on the sides of roads. Brodie knew it was a project close to Trevor's heart and if it was received well in Florida, he wanted to expand nationwide in an effort to combat climate change. He was trying to better the world and Brodie liked working for someone who actually gave a shit.

"Much better. She's resting now." He hated how sick she'd been, how miserable. This morning her face hadn't had that gray pallor. Instead, her cheeks had been the same bronze as before with a slight flush of pink he found…intoxicating.

"Good. I hate that she had food poisoning. Does she have any idea what caused it? Antoine is convinced she didn't get it here."

"Not really. She had some cereal, cookies, nothing really of substance. I'm guessing the cookies, since it was the last thing she ate and no one else touched them. I had one of the guys toss them. But nothing that should have come in contact with salmonella or anything." Though if Antoine hadn't wiped down the countertop thoroughly, it was possible. "Also, she's not quitting."

Trevor shoved out a sigh, his shoulders relaxing. "Thank God. My mom's enjoying Oliver right now but I can't put all the responsibility on her, and Patience has been incredible."

Brodie had started to respond when Antoine, Trevor's in-house chef, stepped into the kitchen, carrying a bottle of wine.

He nodded politely at the two of them as he headed for the pantry. But he paused at the door. "How is the nanny?" he asked, his French accent barely discernible.

"Patience is doing well," Brodie answered. Calling her the nanny sounded kind of dick-ish. And he didn't like it—she had a name.

Antoine simply nodded, his expression reserved as always. "Good. She's so wonderful with Oliver. Look…I've checked the expiration dates on everything and I've thoroughly cleansed the countertops—like always—and every surface in the kitchen I can think of. I also tossed any leftovers just to be certain. But I don't think she got food poisoning here." He seemed almost offended at the idea. Which Brodie could understand; the man was a master of his craft.

Brodie nodded. "That's good to hear." He'd assumed Antoine would do a deep clean, but he was glad to have it verified.

"I know she's not staying on long-term," Antoine continued, looking at Trevor. "A friend of mine knows someone who's in between jobs. I said I would pass on their information if you're interested."

Trevor nodded. "Just give the information straight to Brodie."

Antoine nodded before placing a bottle of wine in the pantry and heading out.

"I might stop by and check on Patience tonight," Brodie said. He'd texted her to check in, but he wanted to see for himself that she was okay. "Everything is quiet around the house." And he was here later than normal.

"Good. I thought about stopping by but didn't want to wake her up if she'd fallen back asleep. Any news on those threats?" Trevor asked, changing direction.

"There's nothing to them." The "threats" had more or less turned out not to be anything of substance. There were a few agitators angry about Trevor's new planting project who'd ranted on a few social media forums, but no one with enough clout or muscle to do anything other than rail about it online. Some people were simply angry about everything all the time.

"Good. Let's hope it stays that way."

Brodie nodded and let himself out. Instead of going by the cottage, he texted Patience again. *How are you feeling?*

Good, she responded almost immediately. *Had a whole bowl of soup and now I'm resting again. I'll be good to go tomorrow. I've already texted Flora to let her know.*

Glad you're feeling better, he responded. He tried to think of something else to say, but everything felt…lame. So he tucked his phone away and headed home. He'd ended up getting return calls from all of Patience's former employers and everyone loved her—had nothing but glowing things to say about her.

He really wished he could go back in time and un-fuck-up what he'd done. And he really wanted to punch Richard Miller right in his face. Repeatedly. He'd checked deeper into the guy and Patience had been right—Miller hadn't been legally allowed to talk about Patience's employment. So he'd dropped a line to Alice Miller and her attorney to let them do with that information what they could.

It wasn't much, but fuck that guy. The thought of anyone hurting any woman pissed him off, but he'd started to develop protective feelings for Patience. So the thought of someone hurting her? Hell no.

* * *

"Hello!" Flora's voice called out from the living room area.

Patience had left the door to the main house open, knowing Flora was stopping by. "I'm in the kitchen," she said, slightly raising her voice.

The other woman strolled into the room looking elegant as ever. White linen pants, a multicolored flowing top and of course, the sparkly jewelry.

"What is my favorite little man up to?" She set her purse on the counter and made a beeline for Oliver.

"See for yourself," she said, laughing.

He was in his high chair making a big mess of the mushed plums she'd given him, eating half and throwing half over the side. She'd definitely have a mess to clean up later. And the white onesie he was in was pretty much unsalvageable at this point. But he loved the plums and the coolness of the fruit seemed to help with his teething too. She was calling that a win.

"Ooh, what are you making?" Flora sat next to Oliver, giving him kisses on his cheek and making him giggle.

Patience poured milk into her mixing bowl. "I'm making cupcakes for a friend of mine. I'm going to give one to Oliver to see how he likes it." It would be soft enough for him and he didn't seem to have any allergies so far. She was keeping a list of everything he liked for the next nanny—and for Trevor.

"Maybe you'll make an extra one for me too?"

She snickered lightly. "I think I can manage that."

"So how are you feeling, my dear?" Flora headed for the fridge and pulled out a bottle of sparkling water.

"A hundred times better—and eight pounds lighter," she said, snorting.

Flora laughed as she took a seat at the center island and kissed Oliver on the cheek again, much to his delight. He clapped his hands together, making excited sounds before trying to grab her face.

Patience tossed her a wet cloth to wipe his hands before returning to adding ingredients.

Flora started cleaning his hands as she said, "I want to ask how my son is doing, but you won't humor me with gossip."

She cracked an egg into the mixing bowl. "He's doing completely fine as far as I know. I honestly don't even see him that much. He's at work and I'm here with the cutest little guy in the world."

That got a real smile out of Flora, who turned back to Oliver, now running his favorite plastic bus through his plums. "You're right on that count."

At a slight sound, they both turned to find Brodie stepping into the kitchen. He nodded once at Flora, gave her a polite smile before he turned that intense gaze on Patience. And the look he gave her was a whole lot different. For just a moment—just a flash—there was a hunger there, bright and consuming, before he went all professional. Heat slid through her as she watched him—and her heart rate went into overtime.

"I was just stopping by to see how you're feeling." The sincerity in his voice sent a spiral of…a lot of different emotions through her.

At first she'd really hated that he'd seen her throw up—more than once. But she'd gotten over her initial embarrassment because she had nothing to feel bad for. It wasn't like she could help getting sick. "A lot better. The sight of food doesn't make me ill, so I think I'm good."

His mouth curved up slightly as he watched her, and wow, she felt that smile all the way to her toes. She was probably just projecting what she wanted, but she imagined he was amazing in the bedroom. A man who exuded so much raw sexual appeal couldn't suck in bed, right? At least he didn't in her fantasies. And yep, she'd had a couple.

"I'm glad to hear that." He cleared his throat and glanced at Flora, as if remembering she was there. "So...everything okay with you guys?" he asked a little awkwardly. Which made him that much more adorable.

"We're doing great," Flora said, giving him a big smile.

He nodded then and stepped back, disappearing from sight like a ghost who'd never been there at all. She couldn't help but wonder if she'd see him again today—then inwardly cursed herself for caring at all. Only very recently had she been cursing the man in her head and threatening to quit. Now? She really, *really* wondered what he looked like naked. Okay, she'd wondered that before too. Ever since they'd spoken by that taco truck.

"So how long are you hanging out today?" Patience asked Flora as she started adding the paw-print-covered cupcake liners for her dog-loving—aka obsessed—friend Maddie.

"I'm not sure. I have a spa afternoon planned but I might grab brunch with one of my friends before. So...if I had any hope of you and Trevor getting together, those hopes just died." Her tone was wistful.

Patience's eyes widened in surprise. "What?"

"Oh, I'm just teasing you. I love your mom so much and I had ridiculous fantasies of you and Trevor discovering that you had a spark for each other."

She snorted softly. "Trevor is perfectly handsome and kind, but he's like a decade older than me and there's no attraction there on either part."

She raised an eyebrow. "I'm pretty sure Brodie MacArthur is also a decade older than you, and I just saw some sparks fly."

Damn it. She felt her cheeks flush, but cleared her throat and focused on her mixing bowl. Trevor had one of those fancy, ridiculously expensive mixers but she was a little afraid to use it. So she was doing this with her ancient, teal-colored handheld mixer. And it gave her an excuse to *not* look at Flora.

"Nothing to say?"

"I have nothing to say because I have no idea what you're talking about."

Flora laughed softly and Oliver let out a cooing sound. "I know what I saw."

"Look, Brodie was really kind when I had food poisoning. Trust me, I guarantee he doesn't want to get together with the woman whose hair he held back while she was puking her guts up."

Flora wasn't deterred. "He held your hair back? That's so sweet."

"That's your takeaway from what I just said?"

Oliver let out a squeal and pounded his hands on the tray. Clearly he wasn't getting enough attention from the two of them.

She grinned at him. "Are we not paying enough attention to you, sweet boy?"

He babbled something that sounded a whole lot like yes and waved his hands in the air to make his point. She set her mixer down and grabbed a couple more mushed plums. When she set them in front of him, he clapped animatedly.

Flora laughed. "I'm tempted to cancel my spa afternoon and just steal him."

"You do what you want, but I promise we're fine here. So if you're worried about him—"

"Oh honey, I'm definitely not worried about him with you. You are a lifesaver. We are so grateful that you were able to step in this summer." Her expression turned serious. "It eases my mind a lot knowing that Oliver is in such good hands during the day. And I know Trevor will find someone permanent eventually, but we really appreciate you."

"You should be thankful to my mom. I can't say no to that woman."

"Not many people can. Why do you think we have her on all of our fundraising committees?"

She laughed aloud as she started pouring the batter into the cupcake liners. For a brief moment she thought about setting aside a couple extra for Brodie—just as a thank-you for being so kind when she'd been sick.

But...that seemed too weird, right? *Ugh.* She couldn't ask Flora because she knew the woman would tell her to do it. In the end she decided not to.

Even if she couldn't seem to get the man with the dark green eyes and sexy smile out of her mind.

CHAPTER EIGHT

Patience shut the sliding glass door behind her and headed to the guesthouse. The walk across the property was certainly no hardship. There was a mini-forest on the west side, and tons of lush greenery surrounded the Olympic-sized pool. At night the place was lit up with solar twinkle lights, making it seem magical.

As she walked around the pool, she could admit that she was hoping to get a peek at Brodie. Maybe even talk to him. Sometimes when she looked out the window of the guest cottage, she could pick out his silhouette among the other security guys who were patrolling. It was crazy but she knew exactly who he was even from far away. He had a specific walk. One filled with confidence—which was sexy as hell.

"Hey." Brodie's deep voice startled her as he stepped out from behind a big cluster of bird-of-paradise plants, the oranges and purple bright against the setting sun. He held up his hands, one of which had a bottle of wine in it. "I didn't mean to scare you. I was trying to let you know I was here. I was just on my way to see you."

She smiled, butterflies taking flight inside her because he'd been coming to see her specifically. But then she chastised herself. He was probably coming to see her about something work related. "No problem. You're very quiet."

He fell in step with her. "I hope this is okay, but I got you a bottle of wine." He held it out and she recognized the brand.

"Ah...it's my favorite, so it's definitely okay," she said, laughing lightly. "Are you psychic or something?" She kept her tone teasing even though she was curious how he'd known this. It seemed like too much of a coincidence.

His mouth curved up in a way that made him look boyish and charming and those butterflies were back. Okay, they'd never gone away. "I might have done some sleuthing," he admitted.

"That's a little scary."

"I asked Flora and she found out for me." He looked almost abashed, which, holy hell, this man was twisting her up inside. It should be a crime to be so handsome.

She inwardly groaned because Flora had most definitely called her mom if Brodie had contacted her. There was a teeny tiny chance that Flora had used some discretion but Patience wasn't going to hold her breath on that. "Thank you," she said as they reached the cottage. "This is really nice."

"Look—"

"I swear you don't have to apologize again. We are *totally* fine. I think it's great how protective you are of Trevor and Oliver. I do appreciate this gift though, and since I love the wine, I'm keeping it." She grinned up at him.

He gave her another one of those panty-melting smiles. "Actually, I wasn't going to apologize again."

She let out a burst of laughter. "Okay, you just had that look on your face."

He cleared his throat as they reached her door. "I was actually just going to tell you that if you change your mind about going on a date, after the summer is over, that the offer is still open." Then his eyes did that whole dark and smoldering thing.

Those butterflies were apparently taking up residence in her stomach now. They'd decided that they lived here as long as Brodie was close. She told herself to agree to a date *after* the summer, but she had absolutely no control of her mouth as she said, "We don't have to wait until after the summer."

His eyes heated up even more. "You're sure?"

"It's not like you're my boss." And she didn't want to wait two months to go out with him. Of course things could go epically wrong and then she would have to see him at work and that would be plain awkward, but...she was going to risk it. She was pretty sure he was worth it.

"How about Friday night?"

"I actually have plans with a girlfriend. It's her birthday, but I'm free Saturday."

"There's a festival down by the beach on Saturday. My sister told me about it. Would you like to go?"

She knew which one he was talking about because she'd planned to go. "I'm in."

He half grinned then, revealing that elusive dimple, and she realized his smiles should be illegal too. He looked so tough and capable when he was in "work mode," but now? *Yum.*

"Trevor said you wouldn't be staying here on weekends, so should I just pick you up from your place, or…?"

"Yeah that's fine. I'll get you all the details."

"It's a date." His voice dropped ever so slightly.

Hand on the doorknob, she said, "Did you want to come in for a glass of wine?"

He paused for only a second. "All right. I'm actually off the clock. I was about to head home, so don't feel like you have to share your wine with me."

She snickered slightly as he shut the door behind them. "I didn't say I would be sharing *this* wine."

A deep laugh rumbled out of him. "I see how it is."

She grinned at him, reveling in the chemistry arching between them. Anticipation hummed through her as she thought about their upcoming date and she couldn't remember ever feeling like this about someone. She glanced around as they moved through the living room and was glad the place was neat. Not that she was a slob or anything, but he struck her as the kind of guy who liked everything neat and tidy.

As they reached the kitchen she set the bottle down. "I think there's a bottle opener in here somewhere."

"I've got it." He was at ease in the kitchen, clearly having been in here even before the other night when she got sick.

She sat at the countertop as he moved around with a sexy efficiency, opening the bottle and pouring the glasses for them. She might have stared a little too long as his hands worked the bottle opener—and wondered how talented he was in other things with those long, callused fingers.

"Did you always want to be a teacher?" he asked as he slid a glass across to her. He leaned against the nearby countertop while she stayed sitting.

"No. I changed majors a couple times and realized I was trying to do what I thought my parents wanted me to do."

"Which was?"

"I'd assumed my parents wanted me to follow in their footsteps. My dad was an attorney and my mom managed a couple nonprofits over the last few decades. Every time I looked into business school or anything to do with law, I knew it wasn't right for me. A roommate got me my first nannying job, and after that I knew I wanted to teach. I've been teaching for six years and I love it. Kindergarten is definitely my favorite age. They're so bright and curious. I mean, they continue to be all those things, but kindergarten is that sweet spot. They want to know everything and have so many questions, and I love that wild curiosity."

He laughed lightly. "I've seen you with Oliver and you seem to have a knack with little kids. So what would you be doing this summer if you hadn't been roped into working here?"

"Well, I had a couple trips planned, which I was definitely sad to cancel. I was going to go snorkeling down in the Bahamas with some friends. I recently got my diving license so I planned to do that as well."

"I love diving," he said.

She'd love to see him in nothing but swim trunks. "Something tells me you're a pro at it. I'm definitely still a novice."

He lifted a shoulder. "I've been doing it a while."

Oh, he was definitely a pro and probably too modest to say it. She took another sip of her wine, watching him over the rim of her glass. The dry, fruity flavor burst on her tongue and she sighed in happiness. This was a really nice brand of wine, one she didn't often buy for herself. It was the kind her family usually bought her for Christmas or her birthday.

His radio made a little beeping sound and he frowned. "Sorry, just give me a second." He spoke quietly into it, and even though he was off the clock it was clear he had a small issue to take care of. She fought her disappointment as he put the radio away. "I've got to handle something. I'm sorry to run like this but I'm looking forward to Saturday."

"Me too." And she definitely was. Probably more than she should be. She hadn't been on a date in forever and she couldn't ever remember being so attracted to someone as she was to Brodie MacArthur. There was something about his eyes and smile that drew her in. He had just a hint of wicked about him that made her wonder what was going on in his head.

Saturday couldn't come quick enough.

CHAPTER NINE

"This festival is different than I thought," Brodie said as they strode down the roped-off street.

"How so?" Patience asked, surprised he'd never been. Or at least it sounded as if he hadn't.

A couple blocks along the beach had been completely roped and barricaded off so vendors could set up down the middle of the street. There were tons of food trucks, kites for rent, face painting for all age groups, and in a couple hours a live band would start at one end of the street. The scent of deep-fried goodness filled the air, intermixed with the salty tinge of the ocean nearby. It reminded her of her childhood, so she savored it.

"I've never seen so many people flying kites in one place. Hell, I've never seen so many different types of kites." He glanced over toward the beach as they walked, looking at the kaleidoscope of colors.

Dragons, peacocks, rockets, anything you could think of—the kites were blanketed against the pale blue sky. Thankfully a steady breeze had kicked up all day, making her almost forget the summer heat. Not completely, because that was impossible in Florida.

She snickered softly and took a bite of her churro. "First, I can't believe you've never come, since you've lived here your whole life."

"I don't know how it happened but my parents always took vacations during this festival when we were kids. My sister went for the first time last year and hasn't stopped talking about it. She said something about a kite competition?"

"The kites were originally just for the kids—they used to have competitions to see who made the best one. Now the competition is open to everyone, but it won't be until tomorrow. The ones you're seeing now are just for fun. They've even got rentals for those who don't feel like making one or bringing their own. It's turned into this whole big thing. I think it's pretty cool." They passed a tent filled with different wood carvings of various sea life. She smiled at the artist, recognizing him from all her years coming here.

"Did you ever enter?" Brodie asked.

"Oh yeah. A couple years in a row, but it was pretty clear I lacked any real creativity early on. I never placed or anything."

"So…are you ever going to share your churro bites?" he asked mildly, a grin tugging at his mouth—giving her a glimpse of his dimple. Today he was dressed casually in shorts, a T-shirt with the name of a local fishing charter company and Nikes. It was nice seeing him laid-back like this as opposed to the sexy business suit. She liked both versions of him.

In response, she shot him a sideways glance and grinned.

"Is that a yes?"

She made a biting motion with her teeth then shook her head.

He looked almost startled but then he let out a burst of laughter that took years off his face. "Okay, so Patience doesn't share food. *Noted.*"

"I feel like I should just be up-front about who I am on our first date." And she really hoped there would be a second date. He was so much fun and had been so easy-going and relaxing today. "But I'm in a good mood, so..." She held out the little funnel holding the churro bites.

He snagged one quickly and tossed it into his mouth. Then he groaned. "No wonder you don't want to share. I should have grabbed one myself."

"To be fair, I told you that you were going to want some," she said as they reached an empty bench facing the beach. She motioned, asking if he wanted to sit down.

Thankfully he did, and she practically collapsed on the bench, glad to give her feet a break. She'd definitely worn the wrong shoes today.

"Are you tired?"

"No I'm good." She held out the funnel again. She'd been teasing him about not sharing. Mostly. "I just shouldn't have worn my new sandals today." But they were so pretty and she'd wanted to wear them for their date. Sparkly little gold straps crisscrossed over her feet and wrapped up around her lower ankle. Pretty, yes. But they had no cushion and no heel—no support. So she might as well be walking around in bare feet.

"If you want to head back to the parking lot, we can."

"I'm good, I promise. Besides, we haven't even finished seeing all the vendors. And there's one at the end who sells cute Christmas ornaments. I buy one every year." They were all hand-painted with incredible details.

"You can't have been coming here that long, so how many years is every year?"

"Is that your not-so-subtle way of asking how old I am?"

His mouth curved up and she had all sorts of wicked thoughts. "I know how old you are from your file."

Dammit. She'd forgotten about that thing. "I've been coming here since I was ten and I've been collecting ornaments that long."

"A Christmas fan, are you?"

"Of course. I should probably say something like 'giving gifts is so heartwarming,' and okay, it totally is. I *love* giving gifts—now. But when I was ten, all I cared about was getting stuff. I was such a greedy little thing. I thought if I showed my support for Christmas, Santa would hook me up. And my mom had no idea, she just thought I was this big Christmas fan like her and she loved that I wanted to start collecting Christmas ornaments. Now it's sort of like this bonding thing between us. We buy each other ornaments every year."

"I've actually met your mom—when I stopped by Flora's. She's a trip." Again with the half-smile that did crazy things to her insides.

She blinked. He'd met her mom? And her mom hadn't said anything to her? That was…interesting. She didn't know how to feel about that. "That's certainly one way to put it. What about you? I know you've got a sister but I don't know much of anything else." Flora had mentioned something about him having siblings but she hadn't wanted to be nosy. That was a lie—she *had* wanted to be nosy, but had decided not to be.

"I've got one brother who just got married. Took us all by surprise. Sort of."

"How did he sort of take you by surprise?"

"Well the woman he married, they'd broken up for a while. But it was all a misunderstanding and then as soon as they were back together, he proposed about a minute later, and then two months after that he was rushing her down the aisle."

"Sounds intense." She ate another churro bite, savored the sugary goodness.

"When my brother wants something, he goes for it." He looked at her then, his gaze smoldering and intense. God, what was he thinking right now?

She felt that look all the way to her toes and had the urge to lean over and kiss him. She'd never been one to make the first move on a date, but she was really, *really* tempted. She cleared her throat. "So what about your sister? The one who called you downtown that night we first sort of met."

His expression darkened slightly. "My sister is always in…intense situations. She drives me crazy."

"Why?" She offered him another churro bite, and when he declined she popped one in her mouth. These things were like little bites of heaven.

"Because she's my little sister and I'm probably way too overprotective. She's a PI and always seems to be in danger."

"If she was a man, would you feel as worried about her?"

"I'm going to be honest and say no. And not because Sienna can't take care of herself, because she absolutely can. But the world is not kind to women. And I hate that. I hate that she has to worry about more things simply because men can be assholes."

She nodded in approval. "True enough." She knew that firsthand.

"Can I ask you something?" There was a hint of...some emotion she couldn't define in his voice.

"Yeah."

"If it's too personal, tell me to screw right off."

Oh, she thought she knew where this was going. "Is this about Richard Miller?"

"I...kind of. I found out a little more, and for the record, he wasn't allowed to talk about you. I let his wife and her attorney know."

She raised her eyebrows slightly. "Wow. Thank you. Long story short, he always gave me a creepy vibe. But he was gone all the time, traveling for work, so I took the job. I loved his wife and honestly didn't understand why she put up with him. She had a blind spot where he was concerned. I think we all have them."

He nodded, quiet as she continued.

"Anyway, he lost his job and was supposed to be job hunting but instead spent all of his time trying to talk to me—in front of his kids. I mean, if he wasn't going to be working, I don't even know why I was there at all. I was getting ready to put in my notice because it had gotten to be unbearable to be in the same house as him." He'd been like this lurking shadow. Always there. *Ugh.* "All I wanted to do was work and it was like he wanted all my attention on him. The only reason I stayed was because of the kids. He didn't pay any attention to them, treated them as if they were an inconvenience... You sure you want to hear all this?" It felt heavy for a first date.

As the waves crashed in the background and people milled down the sidewalk behind them, he nodded. "Yes, but only if you want to talk about it. I probably shouldn't have asked."

"It's okay that you did." She was glad to be able to tell him this part of her past. She'd moved on from it and didn't have nightmares anymore. People were passing by them so quickly she wasn't worried about people eavesdropping either. Everyone was caught up in their own world, herself included. "One day the kids were napping and I was doing dishes. He cornered me in the kitchen and made a pass at me. A blatant one. I told him to back off and he tried to act like I was overreacting and reading into things. That he was just being friendly."

She rolled her eyes as she remembered how offended he'd acted.

"I snorted and told him that would be my last day. He looked almost panicked and just attacked. I wasn't prepared for it but I managed to get him off me and bash him in the head with a pan I'd just washed. Then one of his kids woke up, which seemed to startle him even more. He ran out of the house, I called the cops and..." She shrugged. "There's more to it than that, but luckily his wife believed me and left him. And the cops handled everything professionally, so I call that a win too. It was easy for her to get full custody—he actually didn't even fight it, from what I understand."

"I think I know, but why isn't he in jail?" Brodie's jaw was tight and she could see the anger simmering under the surface—at Miller, not her.

"He attacked me but he didn't do any real physical harm. I mean, I have no doubt he planned to rape me. He was absolutely crazed. But it never got that far and it was a 'first-time offense.' So." She lifted a shoulder. "It's not okay what happened, but I can't change the outcome so I made the decision to move forward and not let anger consume me that he's out walking around like he did nothing wrong. If he hurts someone else, it's on him—and our crappy justice system."

He watched her for a long moment, then reached up and surprised her by cupping her cheek gently. "You're incredible."

She blinked even as she flushed at his soft touch. "I don't know about that."

"You are. Thank you for sharing all that with me. And I know I'm not supposed to apologize again—"

"Then don't." She'd enjoyed today and didn't want any more apologies, didn't want to dwell on the past anymore. She wanted to live in the moment with him.

Brodie's mouth quirked up slightly. "All right." He still cupped her cheek, watching her for a long moment before he cleared his throat and dropped his hand. "Hey, do you mind sitting tight for a couple minutes? I wanted to grab some more of those churro bites. I'll grab you another funnel too?"

She grinned slightly, the weird band around her chest easing a bit. She was glad she'd told him all that, felt almost relieved to get it out there. "I'm actually good, but thanks." She crumpled up her little funnel cake holder and handed it to him as he stood. "I wouldn't mind some water though."

He nodded and hurried off—and she totally checked out his ass as he walked away. Because the man had a seriously fine one. A nice, perfect bubble butt she wanted to grab onto. *Gah.* She'd never felt such an intense reaction to someone and it had her off-kilter. Brodie had her off-kilter in general.

Tearing her gaze away from the fine man, she stared out at the kites and felt more relaxed than she had in ages. She wasn't sure how much time passed but eventually he returned and she frowned when she saw he was carrying a brown bag and the food. "What's this?" she asked as he sat and handed her the plain bag.

"It's those wind chimes I saw you admiring earlier. I passed them on the way to grab the food." He shrugged as if it was no big deal.

But that vendor wasn't anywhere near the food carts so he'd gone out of his way to get this for her. Her eyes widened slightly as she peered inside. "Brodie, that's incredibly thoughtful. Thank you." She wanted to tell him that they had been way too expensive, which was why she hadn't even thought of buying them when she'd seen the price tag. But she didn't want to insult his gift either. And…they were gorgeous. "Seriously, this is so generous, thank you."

He lifted a shoulder but she could tell he was pleased by the small grin that played across his face. Wicked, wicked smile. "I'm glad you like it."

Patience stared at him for a long moment, then suddenly they both moved into action. She wasn't sure who leaned forward first, her or Brodie. But they were staring at each other and then suddenly they were kissing, his mouth on hers, dominating and teasing at the same time.

She leaned closer, the bag crinkling between them as she grabbed onto his shirt and tugged him closer.

He tasted sweet like the sugar from the churro, and when he gently bit her bottom lip she moaned into his mouth. The way his tongue flicked against hers sent spirals of pleasure rolling through her as she wondered if he'd be talented with that tongue in other ways.

God, she could straddle him right here, just move and slide her legs over his, roll her hips against his. And at *that* thought, she slightly straightened and pulled back at the same time he did. Heat pooled low in her belly and it took a moment to get her breathing under control.

His breathing was as uneven as hers as he watched her with hungry eyes. "We'll probably get written up on indecency charges if we keep doing this," he murmured.

That pulled a laugh out of her, easing all the tightly coiled sexual energy inside her. Sort of. "Probably. I'm also debating whether I care or not."

He let out a startled laugh then and grinned at her before popping another sugary bite into his mouth. "I had fun today," he said a few moments later.

"Me too. The day's not over though." She definitely wanted a repeat of that kiss, only a much longer one in private. "I still want to check out the Christmas vendor if you're up to it."

He gathered their bags, carrying all of them, and took her hand in his as if it was the most natural thing in the world.

Surprise flickered through her, but she liked the feel of his callused fingers holding hers. Liked being with him in general.

It almost felt like they were a real couple. Yes, she knew she was getting ahead of herself, so she stopped that train of thought right then and there. She liked Brodie. Way too much. But she'd been wrong about men in the past, so for now, she was just going to enjoy the day and not focus on the future or anything else.

CHAPTER TEN

Patience realized she was humming to herself as she slid the cupcakes into the oven. She felt like some kind of cartoon princess, making cupcakes and singing to herself, and it was ridiculous. *She* was ridiculous. But she couldn't stop smiling and had been since Saturday. Brodie had taken her back home, kissed her again—and made it clear he'd wanted more, but had respected her decision not to take it further than a kiss—and even though she hadn't seen him since then, they had been texting. He'd been working at Trevor's office all day and she could admit she missed seeing him.

And kissing him.

It was probably better that she wasn't distracted by him at work though. So here she was on Monday, making cupcakes for another friend—it was her specialty and her friends always begged her to make her special cream cheese cupcakes—while Oliver was sleeping.

"What are you doing?" a male voice demanded.

She glanced over her shoulder as she set one of the mixing bowls in the sink to find Antoine the chef looming in the doorway. "Making cupcakes." Seemed pretty obvious what she was doing.

He frowned as he stepped into the room. He had on linen slacks, a loose linen tunic, and his blond hair was thick and sun-kissed, making him look more like a surfer than a chef. He was only a few inches taller than her, but had a presence that made him seem bigger than he was. "You have a kitchen in the guesthouse," he said tartly.

Surprised by his rudeness—but not going to feed into it—she looked away from him and turned the water on hot to start cleaning the dishes. As she did, she glanced at the monitor. Oliver was still sleeping soundly.

"Excuse me, did you hear what I said?" She could feel him moving up behind her and on instinct she tensed.

But she wasn't going to flinch and let her fears based on the past take over. This guy was harmless and clearly wanted to argue with her. But she worked with kindergarteners on a daily basis. She was so not getting into anything with him. She added soap to the sponge. "I heard you, but I'm not sure what response you want. I'm making cupcakes while Oliver is sleeping, and I'm not in your way." What was with this guy?

"Must be nice having a job where you can slack off," he grumbled as he stalked toward the pantry door.

Holy hell. Something had crawled up this guy's ass, apparently. Or maybe he was always a dick. She chose silence instead of engaging in dialogue with him. She'd learned that was sometimes the best way to defuse any situation. She started washing the dishes she'd used and setting them onto the drying rack next to the sink.

"You better not have used any of *my* ingredients."

Okay, enough was enough. She shut off the water and turned to face him as she wiped her hands on the gray-and-white checkered dish towel. "Trevor said I could use this kitchen anytime I want. He even said I could use *any* ingredients in here—but I used my own. Oliver is very clearly sleeping," she said, jerking her finger over her shoulder at the monitor. "If you have a problem with me being in here, take it up with Trevor. Otherwise, you better back off."

His eyes widened slightly and it was clear she'd surprised him. Maybe he was just a big bully, and while she didn't want to buy into stereotypes, on all those chef shows the chefs were always kind of jerks. Always yelling at people.

He let out a huffing sound. "Just stay out of my way," he snapped before he turned on his heel and literally stomped from the room. Like a toddler.

Well, then. She would definitely be staying out of his way. He must be really good at what he did for Trevor to put up with that kind of attitude. Though something told her that he didn't act like that to his boss. No, she'd learned that some people showed their true colors to those they assumed couldn't do anything for them.

When she heard a rustling sound on the monitor, she turned to find Oliver waking up and rubbing his eyes.

She glanced at the oven timer and hung the dish towel over the lip of the sink before hurrying from the kitchen. Time to get back to work.

* * *

Hours later and finally off the clock, Patience realized she was humming to herself yet again as she pulled into the parking spot of the specialty lingerie shop. "Cut it out, girl," she muttered to herself.

She'd never been here before but several friends had mentioned the place, and something told her that if she and Brodie continued down their current path, she was going to want to have some sexy undergarments on hand. Though he was a guy and probably wouldn't care about her plain black bra and underwear. But screw it, she wanted to feel sexy and feminine for herself. Okay, for him too. She wanted him to like what he saw if and when they got naked. At this point she was pretty sure it was a "when." At least on her end.

An hour later, after spending way too much money, she deposited the two black-and-white striped bags into her back seat. They joined the bag of specialty coffee she'd bought for Brodie. She'd been sneaky and asked Flora what he liked, and to her surprise the woman had told her. And Flora also hadn't teased her or anything about her interest in Brodie.

She was still annoyed by the way Antoine had acted toward her today in the kitchen earlier, even though she'd tried to brush it off. She'd had a great day with Oliver—playing in the pool with him, and Flora had dropped by for another visit—and then Trevor had gotten home early so she'd taken off to run some errands, including dropping off those cupcakes to her friend.

And now she needed to take her bags back to her house instead of the guesthouse. Because if anything was going to happen with her and Brodie, it certainly wasn't going to be at the guesthouse. That felt waaaaay too weird. Technically it was her private quarters but it was still where she worked, and she wasn't going to be hooking up with the head of security there.

If she even hooked up with him at all. *Dammit.* She had to stop getting ahead of herself. They'd been on *one* date—one really fun date. And they'd shared a couple kisses. And a lot of texts. Even though she tried to tell herself that she needed to slow down, it was hard to when she was extremely curious what the sexy man looked like naked. Because the man could kiss. She'd always thought that kissing was an extension of other things. He'd taken his time, been teasing and sweet, but she'd been able to feel raw energy humming through him as she'd clutched onto his arms. He'd been as amped up as she was.

Yep, she had to stop this train of thought now before she worked herself up.

As she turned onto the next street, she frowned when she saw the same car behind her that she'd seen back at that coffee place. She swore it was the same black sedan because it had a yellow sticker in the same place. Whoever the driver was could just be going to the same place as her, but it felt weird because she remembered seeing the same vehicle hours ago. It was after dark…and maybe she was letting her imagination run away with her. She watched a lot of true crime shows, and the truth was, after what had happened with Miller, she was more vigilant about her surroundings.

As she came to a four-way stop, she started to slow. The car behind her sped up, ramming into her.

Her head snapped forward as her car flew into the middle of the intersection.

Heart in her throat she pressed the gas, wanting to get away from this lunatic. She'd sped forward, flying through the intersection, when flashing blue lights came out of nowhere. She started to pull over when the car behind her reversed and raced off in the other direction.

The blue lights got brighter, obscuring her vision, so she flipped her rearview mirror up even as her heart rate increased. Why wasn't the cop chasing after that driver?

Feeling disoriented, she rolled down the window as a female officer approached her vehicle.

"Ma'am, are you okay?"

"Yeah... Shouldn't you go after him?"

"I've already called it in," she said, crouching down by Patience's open window. The woman's blonde hair was pulled back in a tight bun, highlighting sharp cheekbones. Her name tag said *Officer Kaminski*. "My partner is a few blocks back and he'll pick the guy up. Are you sure you're okay? Do you think you can step out of your car?"

With trembling fingers, she unstrapped as the officer opened the door for her.

"It looks like your bumper is demolished," the officer said, wincing slightly as they reached the back of Patience's car.

Sighing, she rubbed a hand over her face. She was going to have to make a report, call her insurance and deal with a bunch of stuff she didn't want to. She was grateful to be okay, but this still sucked. Who the hell had that asshole been, and why had they hit her? For the briefest moment, she thought of Miller getting word about who she was working for. Was it possible he'd come after her when Brodie tipped off Alice about what he'd said? No… She wasn't going to read into this and there wasn't remotely any proof that this had been him. Still, the thought lingered in her mind. "It definitely looks like it. So what do you need from me?"

"I'll help you fill out a report, and if you want, I'll call you a tow truck? I think you could probably drive with this, but it won't be safe driving around with no lights at night."

She looked at the back of her car and winced again when the whole bumper fell off. Yep, she was calling a tow truck. "I'll call my insurance first. I have a towing plan."

The woman nodded, and as she headed back to her patrol car, Patience grabbed her cell phone from her purse and started making calls. She contemplated calling Brodie, but he wasn't her boyfriend or anything and they weren't at that level yet. She did text Trevor to let him know she'd be arriving back at the property later and potentially in a rental. She seriously doubted he would be worried about her coming back late, but she still wanted to let him know that she would be a while. Because she was going to need to get a rental. She had that service in her insurance but it was already seven o'clock and she wasn't sure how late rental car companies were open.

The officer walked back up to her as Patience started to call her insurance company. Looked like tonight was going to be a long one.

Part of her almost gave in to the fear clawing her up inside that she had been an intentional target. She was sure that it had been—whoever had hit her had done it on purpose. But it could have just been road rage at some perceived slight she'd committed. It could be anything at all.

Still, she swallowed back the bubble of fear that dug in and started to take root.

CHAPTER ELEVEN

Patience frowned when she saw Brodie's phone number on her screen. Without pause, she answered even as those familiar butterflies started up their dance once more. "Hey."

"You were in an accident?" he asked immediately.

"Yeah, sort of. I'm dealing with it right now. I just let Trevor know in case I came back to his place in a different vehicle. I didn't want to surprise your security team rolling up in something else."

There was a pause. "You could've called me."

"I didn't want to bother you. I know you were at the office all day." And okay, they were in a very new stage of their relationship—they weren't even really defined as anything. They'd been on one date.

Another pause. "Where are you now?" After she told him, he continued. "I'll be there in ten minutes."

Before she could respond, he'd already hung up. *Okay, then.* She would be waiting for him.

She rubbed her temple as the tow truck guy strode up to her. "Did you get everything you need out of your car?"

"Yes, thanks." She had her shopping bags, purse, and a few things from her glove box she hadn't wanted to leave. "And you're going to take it to the auto body repair shop on Loch Ness Road, right?"

"Yep. I know the owner. I've been there a few times."

Good, one less thing she had to worry about. She knew the owner too and it was where she normally got her car serviced. Thankfully her insurance company had been fine with her using his company for the repair. They were closed but he was going to leave it in the parking lot and she'd stop by tomorrow with her keys so he could work on it.

"So did you catch the guy?" she asked as Officer Kaminski approached. "Do I need to press charges or anything?"

The tow truck driver had already jumped up into his vehicle and had the engine running. Patience stepped away, walking along the side of the road toward the officer as the driver pulled out, her sad car in tow.

This was a residential area and fairly quiet. She was really close to her home, could probably walk home if she wanted. And right about now she was thinking about doing just that. She wouldn't because Brodie had told her he would be here soon. The rental car company hadn't gotten back to her so she was just going to head to her house instead of Trevor's and Uber to work early in the morning.

"No," the woman said, her expression clearly frustrated. "I don't know how he slipped us but it's like he disappeared. I ran the plate but it's coming back as not in existence."

That...wasn't good. "I'm just glad no one was hurt, myself included." The road had been nearly deserted when he'd hit her. The cop had been idling underneath a cluster of bushes by the stop sign, very well hidden. For that she was very grateful, because if that jerk had targeted her because she was a single woman alone in a quiet area, things could have gone very differently.

"So what's going on with your insurance company? Do you need a ride? I thought you'd leave with the tow truck driver."

"I have a friend on his way to pick me up. He should be here soon." Or she hoped he would take her home. If not, she'd be Ubering for sure. But something told her no way in hell would Brodie leave her here. Not the man who'd held her hair back as she got sick.

"Well, I'm going to stick around until you get picked up." Her radio sounded so she stepped away and started speaking into it quietly.

Patience pulled out her cell phone and texted her mom to let her know what had happened. Moments later she received a flurry of texts wanting to know if she was okay, even though she'd very clearly said that she was perfectly fine and uninjured. Her mom drove her crazy sometimes but there were certainly worse things than a parent who actually cared.

In the midst of her texting, headlights from the opposite direction of the police car flashed and she instinctively knew it was Brodie when she saw the outline of the SUV.

He pulled off onto the side of the road as she approached the vehicle, and when he jumped out his expression was tight. He scanned her from head to toe in a completely clinical fashion.

"I'm fine," she said, feeling ridiculously better now that he was there. "Promise."

"You're sure?" He ran his hands over her shoulders and up and down her arms as if making sure for himself. And okay, she found that incredibly sweet.

She waved at the officer and motioned that she was heading out. "I'm so ready to get away from here."

He nodded. Moving incredibly fast, he picked up her bags and had the passenger door open for her. She inhaled his masculine, sort of woodsy scent as she brushed against him. Surprising her, he actually strapped her in and she had to resist the urge to inhale deeply.

It was pretty clear that he was the overprotective type, something she'd never thought she'd like. But right now she definitely didn't mind—she kind of liked it. Maybe more than liked it. Years ago she'd gotten into a fender bender and called her boyfriend at the time—definitely an ex now—thinking he would come pick her up. Nope. He'd chosen to stay with his friends because he hadn't wanted to miss the ending of a football game. She'd realized her priority in that moment.

"So what exactly happened?" Brodie asked as he pulled away. "Trevor didn't have many details."

She hadn't wanted to worry anyone. "Some guy ran into me from behind. Seriously, just some giant jackass decided to run me off the road. I thought I'd seen the same car earlier when I was out running errands but there's no way to be sure. The police had someone looking for him but he slipped them somehow. Maybe he lives nearby or something."

"Are you sure it was a man?"

She paused. "Actually, no. I never saw the driver. It was too dark out to see anything. I'm just assuming it was a man." She was fighting the worry building inside her, that maybe this hadn't been a case of road rage. Glad she didn't have to tell him where to go since he'd picked her up for their date on Saturday, she settled back against the leather seat. "I'm sorry I pulled you away from work."

He glanced at her. "It's not a problem. Normally I don't work this late anyway. But regardless, you can call me if you ever have an issue with anything. Even if we're not..." He cleared his throat. "Just, no matter what. Any time of day or night."

Wow. "Thank you." She'd never dated anyone who'd been so...nice. They might have gotten off on the wrong foot, but he was showing her who he was more and more through his actions.

"Did anything weird happen today while you were out? Anyone who you had a difficult interaction with?"

Her heart rate kicked up a bit. "No. And...this feels stupid, but I kept thinking of Richard Miller. I doubt this was him or anything, but I don't know. He was on my mind because of..." She cleared her throat.

Jaw tight, he simply nodded as he pulled into her driveway. Before she'd gathered up her bags, he'd already rounded the vehicle and opened her door. As she slid out, he plucked her bags from her hand—and she was glad that lingerie was wrapped in soft paper so he couldn't see what was inside. The first time he saw it—if he ever did—she wanted to be wearing it.

"I'm going to look into Miller a bit," he said as they approached her front door.

She blinked at him. "What?"

"Did you tell the cops about him or…"

She flushed. "No. Maybe I should have but…" She hadn't wanted them talking to him, hadn't wanted anything to do with that asshole.

Brodie nodded again. "Okay, then I'm going to dig into his whereabouts. I want to know where he was tonight."

"Thanks." A weight she hadn't realized had been pressing on her chest lifted.

Once they were inside, he set all her bags on the kitchen island while she disarmed her security system. She felt tense, her neck and shoulders a bit sore, and she wondered if it would be worse tomorrow.

"I love this place," he said, pointing to the logo on the outside of the coffee company bag he set on the countertop. "I buy all my coffee there."

"I know," she said, flushing. "You're not the only one who can be a sleuth. I found out what your favorite type of coffee was and I was going to surprise you with it. It's for you. I hope that's okay?" It felt kind of weird to be getting him a gift because she wasn't sure what stage they were at. But he'd gotten her those wind chimes, so whatever this was, she'd decided to throw out most of her rules where he was concerned. She'd wanted to do something nice for him, so she had, simple as that.

"That's really thoughtful. So can I have it now, or…" He grinned and she felt it all the way to her toes. He should definitely smile more often.

She snickered. "Go ahead. I was going to give it to you for our next date, but now is just as good a time as any."

"What's in the other bags?"

Heat infused her cheeks as she thought of the silky, skimpy bralette and thong set she'd bought. The pale blue bralette gave absolutely no support and was definitely just for looks. It had ties at her shoulders and the thong had ties at her hips—and she'd definitely bought them with him in mind. Yep, she'd imagined him slowly unwrapping her.

"What's going on in your head?" His voice dropped an octave as he watched her with intensity. "Because I really want to know what's in those bags now."

She cleared her throat. "Just girl stuff."

He eyed the striped bag. "Like, dirty stuff?"

"Put it this way, if you're lucky, you'll get to see me wearing what's inside."

His dark green eyes practically went electric at her words. "I hope I'm a lucky man."

Oh, she had a feeling that he was definitely going to be lucky. And that meant she would get lucky too if he was the giving type of lover.

Something told her that he would be. She really, really wanted to find out. She felt like she knew him so well already, but had to remind herself that they'd only been on one date—and she didn't want to jump into anything too soon and ruin what they could have.

CHAPTER TWELVE

"Boss, I think you need to get to the kitchen." Angelique's voice came over the radio comm line, her words clipped. The petite martial arts expert was one of his best security contractors.

Brodie recognized that tone. "On my way." He'd been checking out a potential disturbance along one of the hedge lines, but it only took him a couple minutes to make it inside the house.

"I know she took it!" Antoine shouted.

Before he stepped into the kitchen he heard Angelique calmly speaking to Antoine, and Oliver fussing. His heart rate increased as he entered the kitchen to find Patience holding Oliver against her chest, rubbing his back as a red-faced Antoine glared at her.

"What's going on?" Brodie asked as he looked between them.

"She took it," Antoine shouted again. "I know she did." His whole body was vibrating with rage.

It was very clear to Brodie that Patience was fighting back tears. Her Mediterranean blue eyes shone with them as she looked at him, rocking Oliver now. It took everything in him not to snap at Antoine for upsetting her. She'd already been through enough after that asshole hitting her last night—at least Miller didn't seem to be a threat. He'd been logged flying out of the state a week ago for work and hadn't returned.

Jaw tight, he strode fully into the room, putting his body between hers and Antoine's as he faced the chef. "I'm only going to tell you this once." His words were clipped and even. "You need to stop yelling. You are very clearly upsetting Oliver—*Trevor's* baby. If you raise your voice again, I will escort you off the property. What the hell is wrong with you?"

Antoine took a deep breath and nodded, but his cheeks were still flushed an angry red.

Brodie turned around and looked at Patience, who seemed to have blinked away the tears. God, he wanted to comfort her. "Are you guys okay? Do you need to take Oliver somewhere else?"

Oliver was now sucking on his thumb and had his head curled up against her neck, clearly having calmed down. "He's fine now," she said quietly, continuing to rub his back.

"Let's start at the beginning. What's going on? What do you think she took?" Brodie turned back to Antoine.

For a moment, Antoine looked as if he was going to yell, but took another deep breath. "She's in here all the time, messing with my stuff. I had some very expensive truffles I was saving for a recipe for Trevor on Friday. Now they're missing. And so is a *very* expensive bottle of wine." He sniffed once. "I brought it up here from the wine cellar a couple hours ago and now all of a sudden it's gone." He glared over Brodie's shoulder at Patience.

"I didn't take anything," Patience said tiredly as if she'd already told the man more than once. "Look, just go check the guesthouse and my car... Ah, never mind. My car's not here." Her expression was one of exhaustion as she continued. "I have nothing to hide."

Brodie knew she hadn't taken anything and didn't want to check at all. But he nodded once, keeping his professional expression in place. Then he looked over at Angelique, who had a grim expression as she watched Antoine carefully. "Keep an eye on him."

Angelique nodded and he had no doubt she would. An Air Force vet, she was exceptionally trained in defusing situations and had a ridiculous amount of martial arts training. But she was small in stature and had a soft look about her—with big eyes and long dark hair she often wore in a braid that made her look younger than she was. People never saw her coming when she took them down.

He'd been trying to keep his distance from Patience all day, not wanting to invade her personal space while she was at work. He wasn't sure what they were at this point and it was too soon to ask her. He gave her a small smile he hoped was reassuring before he hurried out of the room.

Once he was inside the guesthouse, he started in the kitchen since it seemed the most likely place. But when he found the bottle of wine and truffles sitting neatly on a pantry shelf—just out in the open—he frowned.

This was ridiculous. There was no way she'd taken this and then told him to come check the guesthouse when it was in the most obvious place ever. It wasn't even hidden, not really. If she wanted to hide it, she would've put it under the bed or under her mattress, or hell, anywhere but the dumbest hiding place in the world.

He grabbed the bottle of wine and truffles and tucked them into a box of oversize garbage bags. Then he closed the pantry door and started timing himself. He figured he'd give it ten minutes before returning to the kitchen.

Once the time passed, he stepped back into the kitchen.

Patience was leaning against the countertop farthest from Antoine and the monitor next to her showed Oliver sleeping in his crib. Good, he didn't want this jackass anywhere near Oliver at this point. Didn't want him near Patience either.

"Well?" Antoine stepped forward.

"Well what? There's nothing there. She didn't take it."

The man's eyes flared in true shock. And *that* pinged on Brodie's radar. He was way too shocked that Brodie hadn't found anything—because he'd been expecting him to find it.

"You're a liar!"

"Excuse me?"

"I know you're sleeping with her. I see the looks you two share. You're just covering for her!"

Patience let out an angry growl. "He is not!" She stepped forward, hands on hips. "I didn't take anything, you big bully. I don't know what's wrong with you, if you're always this miserable or—"

"Patience," Brodie said quietly.

Her jaw tense, she looked at him, eyes flared with indignation.

"Why don't you head out of here? Go wait in the living room?"

It was clear she wanted to argue with him but she snagged the monitor and left.

Once they were alone, he turned to Antoine. "You're going to take the next two days off and calm down," he said. And in that time Brodie was going to dig into Antoine a bit more. Something was clearly going on with him, and planting stuff at her place was flat-out malicious. It also made him wonder if there was more to the other nannies quitting now. Maybe he'd been bullying them.

Antoine's dark eyes widened, his chest puffing out like a freaking peacock. "You're not my boss."

"No, I'm not. But I handle all of the security here. And it's pretty clear that you are becoming a threat. You need to go home and calm down. Trevor isn't here and you don't need to be here anyway. Enjoy the paid time off."

It was clear that Antoine wanted to argue, but he sniffed and went to one of the drawers. He pulled out a rack of knives and looked at Brodie, as if daring him to argue with him. "These are my *personal* knives. I'm taking them with me so she doesn't steal them too."

Brodie simply sighed and nodded. He knew they were the chef's knives. Everyone did. The man was obsessed with them.

He subtly nodded at Angelique to make sure she followed Antoine off the property. Moments later he found Patience sitting in the living room by herself, her shoulders tense.

She sprang to her feet when she saw him, clutching the monitor in her hand. "Brodie, I didn't—"

"I know. Take a deep breath. He's gone for the next two days. You're not going to have to deal with him. I'll get all this sorted out."

At his words, she let out a huge breath. "He's such a bully," she muttered even as she sat back down on the couch.

"Are you okay? Can I get you anything?"

She shook her head. "No. Just thank you for believing me."

He nodded once even though he wanted to say more. He wanted to talk to her about what he'd found—to pull her into his arms and comfort her—but first he needed to tighten up security and figure out how Antoine had gotten into the guesthouse unseen. "We're going to talk about this soon, but for now just hang tight in the house with Oliver. No one will bother you the rest of the afternoon."

She looked up at him from the couch, watching him with trust and a whole mix of emotions that punched right through him. He'd fallen for Patience faster than he'd ever thought possible. She was sweet and funny, and when he thought of the future, she was in it. Hell, she consumed his every waking thought. He'd never seen her coming.

And he was going to figure out what the hell was going on and why Antoine had clearly tried to set her up. She was his to protect.

***

Hours later, Brodie found Patience in the kitchen, making a grilled cheese sandwich. A woman after his own heart. Trevor was out of town for a couple days so Patience was staying in the house at night in the room next to Oliver's.

"You got a couple minutes?" he asked.

"I have a lot of minutes," she said, smiling. Her long, dark hair was pulled up into a ponytail and she had on small studs in her ears—he'd noticed she wore those with Oliver but on Saturday she'd worn big, sparkly hoops. "Oliver is asleep and it's likely he'll sleep all the way through the night. Since Trevor's gone, I'm about to binge-watch some bad television on that big-screen in his living room." She slid the sandwich onto a plate with a spatula. "You want one? I can make another."

She was much more relaxed compared to earlier and he was glad to see it. In her bare feet, she looked happy and comfortable—and he wondered how she'd look in his house. In his bed.

He cleared his throat. "I'm good, but thanks. I wanted to talk to you about everything from earlier."

Brodie didn't like any of it—was now concerned that Antoine was the reason the other nannies had quit. He'd put in a call to the agency he'd hired them from and was waiting on a call back. Hopefully they could give him more insight.

"Okay, I figured this was coming."

"Look, I found that wine and truffles in the pantry of the guesthouse," he said quietly. No one else was in the house right now. His people were all patrolling the grounds like normal, but he'd wanted to wait to talk to her when Oliver was asleep and she was alone. He hadn't wanted to overwhelm her.

Her eyes widened and she nearly dropped the plate. "What?" She set it back down on the countertop, turning fully to face him. "I didn't take those stupid truffles! I wouldn't even know what to do with them. I certainly didn't take his precious wine—"

"I know you didn't take anything. The hiding spot," he said, using air quotes, "was too stupid. I know you're smarter than that."

She blinked once at him. "You think I would be smarter if I stole stuff?"

He lifted a shoulder and motioned for her to sit at the center island. "Go ahead and eat. And yes, I do. Antoine's surprise was far too shocked when I told him that I didn't find the wine and truffles."

"I don't know what's wrong with him. Freaking psycho probably just wanted to get me fired. He's been pretty rude to me a few times," she said as she went to the refrigerator and grabbed a sports drink. "I brushed it off because I assumed it was just his personality."

"He has?" This was news to him. And his security guys kept him apprised of everything that went on here. So that meant Antoine had been sneaky about his actions. This...was not good. And it backed up his hypothesis about Antoine and the women who'd quit.

Nodding, she sat back down and opened the bottle. "Yeah. He didn't seem to like me using the kitchen even though Trevor said it was totally fine. I used the utensils and stuff in here but I used my own ingredients and made sure to wash everything. I've worked with his type before. He's just a bully, seriously. Maybe it's short man syndrome," she said, rolling her eyes.

"What kinds of things has he done?" Brodie asked.

He listened as she went over the couple times Antoine had gotten in her face—every single one she'd been alone with no security around. It didn't surprise him—no way would his people have let that slide.

"The night you got sick, what did you eat again?" he asked as she set the partially eaten sandwich back on the plate.

She froze, her eyes widening. "Antoine gave me a cookie. Personally. Actually, he was kind of nice to me then, which is why when he was rude to me later I was surprised. It was like a Jekyll and Hyde type of situation."

Brodie tightened his jaw, running through different scenarios in his mind. His security team still hadn't figured out for sure how anyone had gotten into the guesthouse without being seen, but the door had been unlocked. And so had one window. Antoine could have timed it. He worked here so it would be easy to watch everyone's security shifts—even if they were often random patrols. But he would have been very careful to avoid the cameras.

Patience stared at him. "You think he targeted me or something? That doesn't even make sense. Why would he want me to get sick?"

Brodie had some thoughts about that but he kept them to himself for now. "Possibly to make you quit—why, I'm not totally sure. Yet. You're staying inside the house tonight, right?" He wanted it confirmed.

"Yeah, until Trevor gets back I'm staying in the room next to Oliver's. His house is huge though. I might get lost." Her lips quirked up and he resisted the urge to close the distance between them and kiss her senseless. He loved her full lips, the way she smiled, how kind she was. Damn, he really was falling hard.

"I'm going to take care of something tonight. I want you to stay inside the house. But I'll be available by phone if you need anything."

"Anything?" she asked, a hint of heat in her words as she cocked an eyebrow.

Oh, she was going to kill him. "I'm on the clock," he murmured. "And technically so are you."

"I know," she said on a laugh, her expression mischievous. "I was just curious what your answer would be."

"What if my answer had been yes to whatever 'anything' is?"

"I guess you'll never know." Grinning, she took another bite of her sandwich.

Yes she was definitely going to kill him, but in the best way possible. Now he had to shelve thoughts of that, because he had some digging to do. He was going to figure out this mystery and make sure Antoine didn't bother Patience again. And if he was a threat, Brodie would take care of that.

CHAPTER THIRTEEN

A couple hours later, Patience slipped out of bed at the soft knock on her bedroom door. Brodie had told her that the place was locked down for the night so she guessed this was him. Still, when she reached the door she said, "Who is it?"

"It's me."

Her stomach muscles tightened at the mere sound of his deep voice. "Is everything okay?" she asked as she opened the door. She had the monitor next to her bed and Oliver hadn't stirred, but maybe something else had happened.

He nodded once, his expression intense in that hungry way that made her toes curl. "I just wanted to say good night," he rasped out.

Oh. "Good night," she whispered.

He watched her for a long moment, his green eyes seeming darker in the dim hallway. When he moved toward her, she stepped forward on instinct, leaning her body into his as he cupped the back of her neck and slanted his mouth over hers.

She arched into him as their mouths collided, savoring the way he took complete control. Heat flooded her entire body from just that one electric kiss—and it took all of her self-control not to climb his body the way she wanted.

Okay, so she barely had any self-control at this point. When he teased his tongue against hers and backed her up against the wall, she hooked her leg around his hip, her foot digging into his back upper thigh. He rolled his hips against her and now she was the one moaning into his mouth. Everything about Brodie turned her on but when he pinned her against the wall like this? The slightly dominant display, the show of strength... She was definitely into this. Into him.

He clutched onto one of her hips even as he kept his other hand firmly in place behind her neck. She wasn't sure why that was so hot, but she loved the feel of him holding her like this. Her nipples beaded tightly as his tongue delved into her mouth, tasting, teasing, taking.

She dug her fingers into his shoulders, never wanting this to stop. But thankfully one of them was thinking clearly.

Him. *Not me.*

Breathing hard, he tore his mouth from hers and stared down at her. "I really did just come to say good night. And I need to leave now."

She let her leg drop from around him even though she *really* didn't want to. Heat was pooled low in her belly—and other places. Just a kiss and she was about to combust. "I'm glad you've got self-control," she murmured.

His mouth curved up the slightest bit. "Barely. But I'm already regretting walking away from you."

"Just for tonight though." She wanted that spelled out clearly. Because this could not be all they had together. Hell no. She wanted to experience all of Brodie MacArthur.

"Just for tonight," he said in agreement, his eyes smoldering.

As he took another step down the hallway, then another, she slipped back into the bedroom and shut the door. Sighing, she collapsed against the bed, her entire body tingling with anticipation of what was to come.

They'd only been on one date and shared a couple kisses, but they had been the most incredible kisses of her life. Where on earth had this man come from? He'd completely disrupted her whole life with that talented mouth and tongue. And his sexy voice.

And his sweetness, thoughtfulness and protectiveness. The texts he randomly sent her throughout the day were cute and seemingly at odds with the man she viewed as so tough and capable.

Her clit pulsed between her legs and yep, she was definitely going to have to take care of business tonight. Otherwise she was going to toss and turn the next few hours in discomfort.

She just wished that Brodie was here with her, and they were both getting each other off. But her hand would have to do for now.

* * *

Patience jogged down the stairs the next morning, feeling ridiculously energized even as worry hummed through her. The events of yesterday still lingered in her mind, but she was still excited about where things were headed with her and Brodie. She shouldn't be, considering she'd gone to bed sexually frustrated last night instead of getting a taste of the real thing—and it had felt way too weird to take care of herself in someone else's bed.

But she was still excited nonetheless, knowing that this weekend she and Brodie were going on another date. And since Flora had texted her, telling her she was coming by early to grab Oliver, she'd let Flora in the house then showered, taken a couple extra minutes under those wonderful jets, dressed in summer shorts and a tank top, and was ready for the day.

When she stepped into the kitchen, she was surprised to find Brodie there with Flora and Oliver. Brodie had on what she'd come to think of as his standard issue "uniform." Black slacks, a white button-down, with no tie. He didn't have on his jacket this morning, however, and his sleeves were rolled up, showcasing the roped muscles of his forearms. *Good morning, indeed.*

Oliver's little face lit up when he saw her and that definitely made her heart squeeze. She was totally going to miss the little guy but at least she knew she'd see him in the future since their families ran in the same circles. He made grabby hands for her so she headed straight for him and lifted him out of his high chair. "Hey, guys."

"Aren't you looking refreshed this morning," Flora said, a twinkle in her eye as she took a sip of her coffee.

Patience was sure there was more to *that* comment but she chose to pretend there wasn't. "It's no wonder. This house is incredible and the beds are like clouds. It's like five-star hotel quality," she said as she kissed Oliver's cheek.

"It's true," Brodie said, a smile tugging at his mouth. "I've stayed over a few nights and I'm always sad to return to my own bed."

"So what's up?" she asked, looking between the two of them. There was something hanging in the air, some sort of weird tension suspended and ready to pop.

"Well, we have a bit of a change of plans this week. I went to Antoine's house last night and the place was empty," Brodie said.

"Like he moved or something?" she asked as Flora took a wiggling Oliver from her. He was apparently done with her and wanted his Nana now.

"As in, I don't think anyone has lived there for a while." Brodie's expression was grim as she moved toward the coffee maker.

"So what does that mean?" She poured herself a cup in what she was coming to think of as "her mug," a blue-and-white striped mug that was the size of her face—perfect for coffee.

"His phone has been disconnected, but I've done some digging into him. When we hired him, he came highly recommended. And until the incident with you, we've never had an issue with him. He's been here years.

But I looked into his finances, and over the last few months it seems as if something weird is going on—and I'm worried it might have to do with Oliver."

She froze, coffee mug in hand. "Oliver?"

"Antoine gets paid very well. But he also has a gambling addiction that's just showed up on our radar. As in yesterday. He's apparently been able to pay off his debts—until recently. Which is why nothing pinged on our radar. I can't say for sure, but with all those nannies quitting so suddenly... Something isn't adding up. Especially since he recommended a nanny to Trevor. Which in itself is fine, but the résumé he gave me is too good. The woman doesn't have much of an online presence, and the references... I'm not buying them. There's a lot of things that are triggering some red flags. So I want to be cautious, especially since Trevor is out of town and Antoine has spent a whole lot of time in this house. And somehow he was able to get into the guest cottage unseen. For now we're going to relocate Oliver to Flora's lake house."

Her heart rate increased as she digested all he was saying. It sounded a whole lot like Antoine wanted to kidnap Oliver—or at the very least he was working with people who did. This was all too surreal. She'd worked for some wealthy clients before but no one on the level that Trevor was so she shouldn't be surprised that someone might try to kidnap Oliver. Still, the thought that someone could take a sweet, innocent—helpless—baby and use him for ransom was terrifying. "What do you need me to do?"

"Honestly, I want you to pack up and go somewhere you feel safe. Flora tells me your parents' house should be safe, but if not, I'll set you up somewhere myself. It's just for a few days. I've already called a friend at the FBI and he's looking into everything. Antoine owes money to some shady guys and if they had plans to kidnap Oliver or rob Trevor's place, we'll find out."

Holy crap, the FBI.

"That's no problem. I'll stay with my parents. But are you sure you don't want me to stay with you?" she asked, looking at Flora.

Flora shook her head. "No. Frank and I will have things under control. I'll feel better knowing he's with me, to be honest," she said as she cuddled Oliver close. "And Brodie is going to have some of his security at our vacation place as well. It's pretty hard to reach, so if anyone manages to track us down there, we'll have plenty of notice and be able to get out."

"Well I'll be a phone call away. You're sure the security will be enough for Oliver?" she asked, looking at Brodie.

He looked amused for a moment and cleared his throat. "Yes, of course."

"Sorry, I'm not questioning your ability to do your job. I just… Now I'm really worried for Oliver." She looked over at him, at his sweet, smiling face.

"It's all good. I understand. We're getting ahead of this to make sure nothing happens to him. I've also set up an SUV for you to use for right now. I don't like that you were in that 'accident' the other night and the driver still hasn't been found. It could be a coincidence, but I don't believe in those."

She went still inside. "Do you think I'm...a target?"

His jaw was tight. "I'm not ruling out the possibility. Do I think you're a real target for kidnapping? No. But I think that you might have been targeted yesterday in an effort to take you out and make room for a new nanny. But all that's shot to shit now so there's no reason for Antoine or anyone else to come after you. Still, I want you holed up and out of sight. It's why I want you in a company vehicle and...I'm going to have someone on you."

"On me?"

"You're going to have security. At least to follow you to your parents' place and...to look after you there."

"I...okay. Obviously I want to be smart about everything." She wished he was going to be coming with her, but knew that would be impossible. He had a whole lot of security issues to deal with now, that much was clear. "Okay then, I guess I'll just pack my bag and head to my parents' now?" She lifted an eyebrow at Brodie, who nodded.

"I'll walk you to the guest cottage."

She gave Oliver kisses and Flora a brief hug before heading out.

"I didn't want to offer in front of Flora, but you are more than welcome to stay at my place," he murmured as they moved around the pool.

Oh that sounded so good. *Way* too good. "I really want to say yes, trust me. But I have a feeling you're going to be working around the clock trying to make sure Oliver is safe, so it's probably better that I stay at my parents'." And she didn't want the first time she stayed at his place to be because of a threat. She wanted to be there because he'd asked her—just because.

"The offer is there. And you can stay in a guest room—I'm not trying to pressure you for anything."

"I know. And fair warning, I'm probably going to pressure *you* if I stay over," she said.

He grinned down at her. "I swear I never know what's going to come out of your mouth."

"Is that a good thing?"

"It's a great thing."

He did some sort of sexy security guy thing and swept the entire guest cottage before allowing her inside to pack her small bag and toiletries. Then, after a very brief kiss in the living room, she was gone, with one of his security guys following after her.

And she was really glad to be driving one of Brodie's company vehicles. The thing was like a tank—and he'd mentioned that it had bullet-resistant windows—so she felt secure inside it in case some other weirdo tried to run her off the road. But she hated what was going on, hated that Oliver might be in any sort of danger. She trusted Brodie to take care of things and understood why he couldn't be with her.

Even if she wished he was.

CHAPTER FOURTEEN

Patience glanced at her cell phone as she headed to her mom's house. When she saw her neighbor Marcy's name on the caller ID, she frowned. Using the vehicle's OnStar system, she answered. "Hey, what's up?"

"Hey, look, I know you're doing that nanny gig for the summer," she said. "I'm sorry to bother you."

Patience had told her neighbors because she wanted them to look out for her house. And Marcy had been wonderful enough to check her mailbox during the week. But at her neighbor's tone, a lead ball settled in her gut. Oh God, had something happened?

"One of the boys knocked a baseball into your back window. It's completely broken. We're totally going to fix it, but I wanted to let you know."

The tension in her belly eased. She was actually surprised her security system hadn't gone off, but...she couldn't remember if she'd set it when she left with Brodie the other night. She'd been so distracted after dealing with the police and her insurance company. And then Brodie's larger-than-life presence in general. "It's totally fine. Actually, I'm only a couple minutes away. I'll meet you out front."

"All right, see you then."

She knew she was supposed to go to her parents', but this should only take a few minutes. She glanced in the rearview mirror and saw the SUV trailing her a few vehicles behind. She figured he'd just follow her.

As she reached her driveway, she saw him park across the street at the curb. *Good.*

She waved at him as she got out. The man, Mac, was as big as Brodie, but he had a head full of red hair and a beard to match it. Plus she'd seen more than a couple tattoos when he'd pushed his sleeves up. He definitely had the intimidating look of what she imagined security people looked like.

She hurried across her yard, ready to get this taken care of. She had tons of boards saved in her backyard shed that she put up during hurricane season to protect her windows. It was just Florida life.

Marcy and Bradley were waiting in their yard as she hurried across the grass. Poor Bradley looked so dejected, his little face turned down as he glanced at his scuffed black-and-gray sneakers.

"Hey guys," she said, smiling at Marcy.

"I'm sorry I broke your window, Miss Patience," he murmured.

"It's okay. Accidents happen. I promise I'm not mad."

He glanced up at her, his expression hopeful. He was only nine and she'd watched him and his brother grow up over the years. She couldn't believe he was so worried about this, but he was still a little kid. "Really?"

"Really. Unless you did it intentionally?"

He shook his head vehemently. "I would never do that!"

"Then it's totally fine. I promise, accidents are no big deal."

"Head inside," his mom murmured.

"So it sounds like you've had a morning," Patience said as she headed around the side of the house, Marcy walking with her.

"I love summer but I also hate summer," she said, laughing. "I told them so *many* times to play ball in the backyard and not here. But they only listen half the time."

She snorted because she understood. It took a long time for kids to grow out of that phase and actually start listening to instructions. She hated it when adults thought kids should act like adults—because they weren't. They were little humans still trying to navigate and figure out the world. And it was a long process. She stopped in front of the broken window and hid a wince. "You weren't kidding, this is pretty bad." A huge hole was in the middle with the glass spidering out in all directions.

"Yeah, he got it good. Ugh. I'm so sorry."

"It's no big deal. I'm just going to grab the board and put it in place for now. But I don't think it's supposed to rain this week anyway." She would deal with the glass shards later too. Right now she just wanted to take care of this and then get to her parents' house.

"I've already called someone and they said they can be out this afternoon."

"Okay, that works. I'm actually not going to stay, but text or call me with the information of whoever is fixing it. And can you make sure you're with the repair person?" Marcy had a key to her house so she could let herself in.

"I will. And again, I'm really sorry."

"Please don't worry about it. And I'm going to pay for this myself. You're collecting my mail for me during the week over the whole summer, which I really appreciate. As long as you can be here when it gets fixed, let's just call this a neighbor tax, okay?" Marcy shook her head but Patience held up a hand. "I'm serious, just accept the invoice and I'll pay it. I promise I'm not worried about this." After the day she'd had, a broken window was no big deal.

"I'm so glad you're our neighbor. I swear, you better never move."

She laughed lightly as she unlocked the fence and headed for her shed. She glanced over her shoulder and waved at the driver of the SUV again. As she turned back around, she shot a quick text to Brodie, telling him what she was doing. She planned to stay only long enough to get the board put in, check her security system, then text Marcy with the code too. She wanted to at least clear the zone for the window and set the rest of the house.

After she had the board securely in place, she headed around the back to make sure the shed was locked up. Once she was done, she hurried around her pool and across her backyard. As she reached the other side of it, her back door opened.

She froze to find Antoine standing there, a small gun in his hand.

She stared in horror as he took a menacing step forward, the gun pointed right at her. "Where's the baby?"

She blinked, completely paralyzed. Oh no. *No, no, no.*

He stepped closer, his face red and mottled. "Don't make me ask again. Where is that brat?"

"I..." she rasped out, rooted to the spot. She tried to find her voice, cleared her throat. "What are you doing here?"

"I'm pretty sure it's clear what I'm doing here, you stupid bitch. You screwed up my payday."

"You want Oliver?" she asked, trying to play dumb and stall for time. The security guy would come eventually. Right? He had to!

"I'm not going to hurt him," he snapped. "Not as long as Trevor pays me what I need." With a trembling hand, he wiped his sweaty brow and glanced around her yard before motioning her toward her back door. "This way!"

She really, really hated that she had a privacy fence right about now. No one could see what was happening. "I don't know where he is. I was sent home. They told me to take the rest of the week off. I'm just a nanny," she said as she slowly stepped toward him and that gun. She should be running from it, but he would just shoot her.

So she went against her instinctive flight nature and trudged across her yard, her feet dragging like sandbags. She didn't know if she was playing this right at all. Because what if he decided she was useless to him now? Then he'd just shoot her. She fought a shudder, but an icy chill settled into her bones, and she started trembling.

Antoine grabbed her upper arm as she reached him and yanked her hard toward him.

Surprised by the sudden show of force, she stumbled, nearly tripping into the doorframe.

"Watch where you're walking," he snarled before slamming the gun against her temple.

She cried out as pain ricocheted through her head. Blinking, she tried to focus, but blood rushed in her ears, terror forking to all her nerve endings. She had to get away from this lunatic.

Antoine grabbed her arm again, yanking her up. She blinked, spots flashing in front of her eyes. "You're coming with me." He propelled her through her house, heading down the hallway and straight for the front door.

Blood streamed into her eyes and she tried to wipe it away but winced in pain.

He was oblivious to anything as he continued hauling her along the wood floors. "I won't be able to get as much for you as that kid, but I will get something."

She wished she had any sort of defensive training but she wasn't sure it would have mattered since he had that gun.

Unable to see well and blinded by the pain, she stumbled forward as he threw open the front door.

Heart racing as they stepped out onto her porch, she was just glad that Marcy was nowhere to be seen. Neither her nor her kids, because that would be an absolute nightmare. But...where was Brodie's driver? She could see the SUV but he wasn't visible. Oh God. Had he been hurt? She'd been depending on him to see Antoine, to help or call in backup.

No, no, no. Sweat poured down her spine and on instinct she tried to yank away from him.

His grip tightened on her arm.

She sucked in a breath as his nails dug into her skin. Everything was happening so fast. Too fast.

"Make a move and I'll just shoot you and take the loss," he growled quietly as they descended the short set of porch stairs.

Nausea welled inside her even as her emotions fractured in all directions. He was doing this in broad daylight, near the street where anyone could see. He had to be insanely desperate, and desperate men did terrible things. Where was he taking her? She was parked in the driveway but she didn't see any other vehicles.

God, why had she stopped at all? She should have just gone straight to her parents' place.

Damn it, where was that guard? If he wasn't going to help her, she had to help herself. She couldn't get into whatever vehicle Antoine had. That was certain death.

Think, think, think.

She had to do something. She knew that when being kidnapped at gunpoint or knifepoint, you needed to escape within the first ten minutes—or something like that. If she didn't, the chances of her dying went up by a whole lot. But she was terrified of being shot if she tried.

As they reached the sidewalk, she saw a four-door green car with tinted windows across the street, parked in front of a neighbor's house. It didn't look familiar.

"Where's your car?" she asked as he tightened his grip again. Then she winced and cried out instinctively at the bruising hold.

"Shut up," he snarled, dragging her across the street.

She looked around wildly, hoping that someone saw, called the police or…something. The sun beat down on her face and even though sweat trailed down her spine, ice still clung to her bones.

She saw movement out of the corner of her eye, but before she could turn, Brodie slammed into Antoine.

The man flew forward. The gun fired. Glass shattered, the car window exploding.

She screamed briefly at the ear-piercing gunshot, but Brodie tackled Antoine against the car with a thud. The weapon flew across the asphalt, skittering into the gutter.

"Get off me!" Antoine screamed as he tried to take a swing at Brodie.

Brodie grabbed his arm and twisted it behind his back as he slammed Antoine against the truck again.

Patience moved into action, racing around the front of the car to pick up the gun. Before she could make it, the broad-shouldered security guy who'd been following her came seemingly out of nowhere and scooped it up with efficiency. Mac quickly tucked it away and started to say something to her, but she turned back to find that Brodie had Antoine on the ground, hands behind his back as he secured Antoine's wrists expertly and efficiently.

"Mac, get over here," Brodie snapped.

The other man took over as Brodie jumped up and pulled her into his arms. "I've already called the police and they're on the way."

She had so many questions— So. Many. But she buried her face against his chest as stupid tears leaked out of her eyes. She didn't even mind the pain from her head as she held on to him tight. She could have died. Been tortured. Oh God. Anything could have happened.

Having Brodie's arms around her grounded her even as she allowed the leash on her emotions to slip. She didn't want to break down here, but she was damn close as he murmured soothing words to her. The only thing keeping her from having a total meltdown was Brodie's strong embrace.

He'd come for her, had been there when she needed him most. Brodie had saved her.

And she wasn't letting him go anytime soon.

CHAPTER FIFTEEN

"This is ridiculous," Patience said as she got off the hospital bed. "I don't need to be here."

Brodie stepped forward, his expression as intense as it had been all afternoon as he gently placed his hands on her shoulders. "You *do* need to be here. They're almost done. The doctor said all she needed to do was get your prescription and then you'd be discharged. I know this sucks."

Yeah, she knew all that. Crossing her arms over her chest—and knowing she was being churlish—she sat back down. And winced at the pulsing pain in her head. Thankfully she hadn't needed stitches and she didn't have a concussion, but they had put a few Steri-Strips on her forehead.

She'd been here for hours since she wasn't considered an emergency and she just wanted to go home and sleep in her own bed. The police and EMTs had asked some questions, she'd filed a police report and had been taken to the hospital for further examination. "Have you heard anything else?" She'd seen Brodie glance at his phone a few times.

Brodie took one of her hands in his, squeezed softly. "Antoine is being officially booked. And the Feds are involved now too. It's a mess, especially since this involves

Trevor. For now, it's out of the media, but that might change."

Sighing, she simply nodded and squeezed his hand back. This was definitely a mess. But she was grateful to be alive and relatively unharmed.

She'd also found out in the previous hours that the security guy Mac had seen movement in her house and hurried to try and warn her—after a quick text to Brodie. He hadn't been able to get to her in time before Antoine had pulled that gun on her. By then Brodie had arrived and they'd worked together to bring the lunatic down. Apparently Antoine owed the wrong type of people a lot of money and had the bright idea to kidnap Oliver to get what he needed from Trevor. Sighing, she rolled her shoulders once, trying to ease some of the tension. Until she got out of here, she knew that it wasn't going away.

"You want me to find out what's taking so long?" he murmured when she didn't respond.

She nodded and smiled. He was such a steady rock right now. "Yeah. Sorry I'm being kind of grumpy." She hated hospitals and she kept reliving how helpless she'd felt at the end of that gun. It had been an eye-opening, horrifying experience that had torn a strip in the fabric of her reality. She knew that no one was ever truly safe, but it was as if her bubble hadn't just been popped, but smashed to bits. Somehow she'd managed to convince her mom not to rush down to the hospital, but only because she'd promised her she would call as soon as she left—and told her that Brodie was with her.

With care, he took her face in his hands and softly kissed her mouth. Just a barely there brush that curled through her, sending little waves of pleasure throughout. It was almost enough to make her forget everything. Almost. "I think you're allowed to be grumpy after all you've been through," he murmured as he pulled back.

She went all mushy at the softness in his voice and in his expression. She covered his hands with hers and smiled up at him. There was a lot she wanted to say, but she would wait until they were out of here.

After he left, she went to look at herself in the bathroom mirror and winced. The doctors had done a good job, but she was definitely going to have a big bruise. And of course it was right on her face for the world to see. Though she couldn't complain. Not since things could have ended up a whole lot worse.

When she heard the door open, she stepped out of the bathroom and found Dr. Shimko stepping inside, a smile on her face. "You're officially good to go. I'm sorry about the wait."

"It's no problem. I know how busy you are." After signing some paperwork—all electronic, thankfully—she tucked her prescription into her purse and tried to text Brodie.

She didn't have service though, so she headed to the nurses' station down the hallway. When she reached the end of it, she froze to find him with his arms around a stunningly beautiful, tall woman. He was smiling down at her with pure adoration and had his arms loosely around her, and the woman—who looked like a freaking model—had her arms thrown around his neck. She gave him a big hug, and when she went in for a kiss, Patience jerked back.

Feeling raw and vulnerable, as if she'd just been sucker punched, she headed toward the elevators. She told herself she was being stupid. It wasn't like he was her boyfriend. They had no official title. They'd just gone on one date.

But...she'd been stupid enough to think there might be something real there. Since she didn't understand how someone could be so caring and sweet and still be seeing other people, kiss someone else when she was right down the hallway... *Ugh.*

A tight ball settled in her gut as she reached the elevators. No way was she going to stay and talk to him. She was just going to go home and text him on her way. She did *not* have the mental fortitude to deal with any of this right now. And stupid tears started pricking her eyes, making her suck in a breath. She would not break down at the hospital.

Nope. Not happening. She wasn't a crier, but right now the accumulation of everything was pushing her down until it was hard to breathe. And she couldn't help but feel betrayed by Brodie even if he hadn't technically done anything wrong. But she couldn't do something casual with him. She wasn't wired that way. When she was with someone, she was with only that person. She didn't do casual dating. She never had. And if that was what he wanted, she wished he'd told her.

Thankfully there was a Lyft driver only a block away and he picked her up in barely two minutes. As the guy pulled away, she texted Brodie as a courtesy, telling him that she was exhausted and had decided to catch a ride home.

He'd probably feel relieved because now he could spend the evening with the stunning model. *Ugh.*

She let her head fall back against the seat and closed her eyes. Soon she would be in her bed and she was going to forget this whole day had ever happened. And probably cry herself to sleep.

CHAPTER SIXTEEN

"What the heck are you doing here?" Brodie asked his sister after she kissed him on the cheek and stepped back.

"It's a long story. Has to do with one of my jobs." Sienna's brown hair was pulled back into a ponytail and she had on jeans, despite the hot weather, and a much too big Ramones T-shirt that was hanging off her shoulder. She'd tied it at her hip, presumably so it didn't hang down to her thighs. It kind of looked like it might belong to a man, because as far as he knew she wasn't a fan of the Ramones.

"Do I want to know?" he asked, eyeing the T-shirt and debating if he should ask if she was dating someone. Because she'd been kind of cagey lately in general.

"Probably not. So why are you here? You look fine."

"You would tell me I looked fine if I had a broken leg." Which she'd actually done before when he'd broken his ankle. Her exact words had been "rub some dirt on it" before she'd taken him to the hospital.

She grinned. "It happened one time and you never let me forget it."

He snorted softly. "I'm here with one of Trevor's employees." Even if he wanted to, he couldn't tell her more than that. Not since it was an open investigation and involved people under his purview.

But his sister didn't miss anything. She narrowed her dark green gaze ever so slightly. "Does this employee happen to be a woman? Because your face just did a really weird thing."

"My face did nothing," he said dryly. "You really need to work on those PI skills."

Completely undeterred, she continued. "Oh my God, have you finally fallen for someone?"

He lifted a shoulder as he felt his phone buzz in his pocket. Thankfully Trevor had been able to catch a flight out and was headed straight to see his parents and Oliver, so he knew it couldn't be him. But it might be his Fed friend with more updates.

His sister started going on about "how the mighty have finally fallen" but everything funneled out as he read Patience's text. He shoved his phone in his pocket. "I've gotta go."

Sienna grabbed his forearm, worry clear in her gaze. "What's wrong?"

"My girl just left."

Sienna blinked. "Oh my God, you really have fallen for someone. Go get her, then."

Heart and mind racing, he hurried out of the hospital and to his vehicle. What the hell had happened? He'd *just* gone to see about her discharge and then she'd...left?

None of this made sense.

The drive to her house took far too long—and she didn't answer his calls, making time stretch to eternity. In reality, the drive was more like twenty minutes. By the time he'd made it there, he'd worked himself up, the fear inside him growing each second that ticked by. Had something happened to her? According to the app he'd installed on her phone—with her permission—she was definitely at her house.

The neighborhood was quiet, and sunset would be here soon, so everything was cast in shadows as he pulled into the driveway.

He knocked on the door once. Then twice. Now real fear settled in and he was feeling irrational enough to kick the door in when it suddenly swung open.

Patience's beautiful blue eyes widened as she stared up at him. "Brodie."

He took a moment to scan her from head to toe, to make sure she was fine—well, as good as could be expected. He hated to see the bruise darkening on her forehead and wanted to pummel Antoine all over again. "Why did you leave the hospital? Is everything okay?"

She rubbed the uninjured side of her head. "I don't want to do this right now."

"Do what? Is something wrong?" For the first time in as long as he could remember he felt unsure of himself. Something had clearly happened to upset her, but he couldn't imagine what he could have done. "Your feelings about wanting to leave the hospital were valid." Maybe she'd thought he'd been dismissive of her need to leave? He didn't think he had been, but he was covering all bases now.

She sighed and he couldn't read her expression at all. "You didn't do anything."

"Then why'd you leave?" He shoved his hands in his pockets.

She wrapped her arms around herself, looking vulnerable and small. "Look, it's not a big deal. I just saw you with that gorgeous woman, and her kissing you. And…I feel stupid saying this, but I thought maybe I meant more to you. But I mean, of course you're free to date other people. We've only been on one date and I don't own you. It was just sort of like a sucker punch and I didn't feel like talking to you or looking at you, to be honest. I just wanted to come home and sleep. So…yeah. I know it was lame to leave like that but…" She shrugged, the action jerky.

"A woman kissing me?" His mind blanked. "Wait, tall, dark hair, smart mouth?"

She narrowed her gaze at him. "I don't know if she has a smart mouth."

"The only woman who kissed me was my little sister. She also patted my head like I'm a puppy. She was at the hospital, something to do with her job. We were both surprised to see each other." Hell, if this was the only issue, then there was no issue. Because he wasn't letting her be alone tonight. Or any other night. Maybe he should be annoyed that she'd jumped to conclusions but she'd just been held up at gunpoint, attacked and almost kidnapped. He wasn't going to pile on because she was a human with human reactions. Her emotions had to be raw right now.

Her arms dropped from around her middle and her expression thawed. "Really?"

"Really," he said, stepping forward to close the rest of the distance between them. He didn't like having this conversation out on her front porch.

"I'm sorry I jumped to conclusions," she murmured, looking sheepish.

"Can we talk about this inside?"

"Of course." Stepping back, she closed the door behind them.

"For the record, I'm not dating anyone," he said. It was definitely time to have this conversation. "I have no desire to date anyone but you. I'm not into dating, for the most part. I mean yeah, occasionally I do, but work usually consumes me. I met you and now thoughts of *you* consume me. You're all I can think about day and night. Honestly I think I have a problem." God, he wanted to touch her so bad right now, to hold her close.

"I'm not into casual dating either," she murmured. "I felt stupidly hurt when I saw you with her. I should have been a freaking grown-up and just talked to you but I was feeling way too vulnerable." She groaned. "And now I feel *really* stupid knowing that she's your sister."

He gently cupped her cheek, was glad when she turned into his hold. "You should never feel stupid. I'm glad you cared enough, but I hate that you left without talking to me about what you saw. You need to be resting right now. I'm going to be taking care of you."

"I see the bossy Brodie is back." Her smile met her eyes now as she looked up at him and he found himself getting lost in the Mediterranean blue.

"I'm not even going to deny it. I like to take control of situations, especially when people I care about are concerned. So I prescribe that you get in bed, and we'll put on whatever TV show you want, and relax for the rest of the night. But only if that's what you want."

"Are you inviting yourself to stay over tonight?"

"Absolutely."

She gave him a full smile then and it was like a punch to his solar plexus. "Okay, then. But you're sleeping without a shirt."

He blinked. "Now who's the bossy one?"

She grinned slightly and stepped forward, wrapping her arms around him.

He gathered her into his arms and savored the feel of her close to him. He'd almost lost her today, almost lost her before they even had a chance to start. He wasn't going to let that happen again. The very thought of it terrified him—she'd come to mean so much to him in such a short time. "If I can't sleep in a shirt, then you're not gonna either."

"We'll see." She laughed lightly but that wasn't a no.

He would take what he could get. And he didn't care if they simply slept tonight with all their clothes on. He just wanted to be with her, to take care of her. To know that she was safe.

He'd fallen so damn hard for her and today had only proved that point beyond a shadow of a doubt.

CHAPTER SEVENTEEN

Patience walked into the kitchen the next morning to the heavenly scent of coffee. Brodie was leaning against her countertop, shirtless, wearing only boxer briefs and looking *very* good in her kitchen. Like he belonged. He had a smattering of hair on his chest and his abs were deliciously cut.

She was so damn grateful he'd been able to stay with her and he didn't seem to be leaving anytime soon. Which was fine with her. Apparently Trevor had told him to take care of her after everything had happened, and he'd agreed. He'd told her last night that he hired capable people and that they could do their jobs while he took care of her.

She'd slept practically plastered to him the entire night, barely making it through fifteen minutes of the movie they'd chosen. She vaguely remembered him turning it off but then she'd crashed hard.

"Morning." His gaze fell to her mouth as she strode farther into her country cottage kitchen.

"Morning. How long have you been awake?"

"Just about half an hour. I tried to be quiet so I wouldn't wake you."

"You didn't." Of course he was thoughtful enough to be quiet. The man had shown her exactly who he was in little ways every time they were together. She walked straight up to him and wrapped her arms around his middle.

He leaned down, hunger sparking in his gaze as he brushed his lips over hers.

There was a minty freshness combined with the coffee. He'd clearly found one of her extra toothbrushes—she'd seen it next to her toothbrush this morning before she'd brushed her own teeth. It had felt…nice to see another toothbrush next to hers. But only because of him.

She smiled against his mouth. "I like seeing you in my kitchen," she said, feeling kind of vulnerable admitting that. Even though he'd told her that all he wanted was her, she was still reeling from yesterday and felt out of sorts in general. Her entire world had shifted yesterday.

"I like being here. So how are you this morning?" He lifted her up onto the countertop with ease, eyeing her bruised head.

Spreading her legs, she pulled him to her and stroked her fingers up his muscled forearms and biceps. The man really was beautiful.

"Much better now." Leaning forward, she tugged him down to her.

When his mouth met hers, she groaned against him. God, she loved waking up to him. Her head ached a bit but she didn't care. Basically nothing separated them now. Certainly not his boxers or her little tank top and sleep shorts.

She was wide-awake and wanted more of Brodie. She wanted *all* of him. They'd had the whole sex talk and both of them were clean and she was on the pill, so if he was ready for more she definitely was. So. Much. More.

He kissed her softly at first, his tongue teasing hers oh so gently until she reached between their bodies. She didn't want soft or gentle. She wanted the dominating, take-charge Brodie this morning.

She rubbed her hand over his hardening length, not dipping underneath his boxers, but cupping him over them. He shuddered, letting out a sort of growl as she wrapped her fingers around his cock—and the man was thick.

He deepened the kiss and reached for her tank top. Cool air rushed over her as he managed to get it over her head and toss it behind them. He barely gave her time to register her state of undress before he cupped one of her breasts.

Then he pulled back and looked down at her, his gaze landing on her breasts. Her nipples tightened under his scrutiny and she couldn't help but love the way he was watching her—as if he wanted to worship her. She'd never had anyone look at her like this, as if she was impossibly precious.

"You're so fucking gorgeous," He teased one nipple, his callused thumb sending out little shocks of pleasure to all her nerve endings as he stroked. "And I've definitely fantasized about you. Ever since that night at the taco stand."

Hearing the truth in his voice, all her little insecurities disappeared. She shoved at his boxers, wanting to see all of him. "I've been fantasizing about you too." Soooo much.

He helped her get the rest of his briefs down his legs and she sucked in a breath as he was fully revealed to her.

Hot damn. "Wow." It was out before she could stop herself. But come on, the man was thick and perfect and needed to be inside her like ten minutes ago. Her inner walls tightened as she imagined how he would feel, thrusting into her.

"You're really good for my ego," he murmured as he tugged her shorts off. Then, taking her by surprise, he slid her to the edge of the countertop and bent between her legs.

Oh, double wow. She moaned as he flicked his tongue up her already slick folds.

He just got right down to it and she was definitely ready for all of him. She slid her fingers through his short hair, holding his scalp as he ran his tongue along her folds, making her mindless with pleasure.

Her stomach muscles pulled taut and heat rushed between her legs as he focused on her clit. She jerked against his face, enjoying how giving he was. And she wondered where he'd been all her adult life.

"Fuck, you taste good," he growled against her.

The reverberations of his words—and his words—sent more spirals of pleasure through her.

He slid a finger inside her, groaned again when he found how wet she was—which turned her on even more. Her inner walls tightened around him as he increased his pressure on her clit, teasing and sucking until she was writhing against his face, about to come apart at the seams.

He shouldn't have been able to learn her body so fast, but he wasn't taking any prisoners. As he worked his fingers inside her, her climax started building, that delicious pressure inside her pushing, pushing. But she wanted him inside her when she came the first time with him. It felt important.

She clutched onto his shoulders, barely able to rasp out, "In me now."

Breathing hard, he lifted her off the countertop and pinned her against the nearest wall as he guided himself to her entrance.

The shocking display of his strength as he held her up was insanely hot. Hell, *he* was insanely hot. His biceps flexed with his movements, his jaw was clenched tight in concentration—and all of it was on her. *For her.*

As he slowly pushed inside her, his neck muscles tightened as he kept his pace slow, steady.

She sucked in a breath as he pushed all the way to the hilt. She'd never felt so full, so turned on. So…connected to someone.

"Are you good?" He brushed his mouth over hers as her inner walls pulsed around his thick cock.

"Just need a second," she rasped out. Because she definitely needed to adjust to his size.

As he kissed her, he reached between their bodies and started teasing her clit with his thumb.

Oh, hell. It was too much.

And that sent her over the edge. Her orgasm, which had already been right on the brink when he'd just been using that wicked, talented tongue, hit fast and hard as he kept up the pressure.

She clutched onto his shoulders, kissing him as she came around him. "Move," she rasped out against his mouth. Her orgasm was a live thing, pulsing through her, wave after wave of pleasure racking her body.

It was like she'd unleashed him with her soft order. He didn't hold back then, started thrusting, over and over, his big body and upper arm strength keeping her in place as he took all of her.

She rolled her hips against him, meeting him stroke for stroke, her own climax fading as he found his.

When he came inside her, it was with a growl of pleasure that was way too sexy. Her body felt like a live wire as his grip on her shifted, as he slowly pulled out of her.

She felt the loss of him immediately, but he cupped her ass, holding her close to him as he stepped away from her kitchen wall—a wall she would never look at the same again.

He started moving through her house, carrying her to her bathroom. She was still coming down from her high and barely knew her own name at this point. She simply clung to him, enjoying the friction of her still-hard nipples grazing against his chest.

"Hold on," he murmured, and she realized he was starting the shower.

She let her legs fall as they stepped inside. He moved under the jets, taking the brunt of the coldness as the water heated up, and she knew in that moment that she was pretty much over the moon for this guy. She wasn't going to say the L word yet but... She was headed that way fast. Like, "rollercoaster with no brakes" fast.

"That was amazing," she murmured as he finally stepped out of the way so they could both get under the warm, pulsing water.

"We're just getting started," he murmured before kissing her again, this time soft and slow.

The promise in his gaze and in his kiss set a new blaze inside her. One that gave her hope for the future. One that definitely involved him.

CHAPTER EIGHTEEN

One month later

"Do you mind if we stop by Trevor's before we head out?" Brodie asked from the driver's seat of his SUV.

"Of course not. Hopefully I'll get to snuggle Oliver if he's awake." A couple weeks ago they'd found the perfect replacement for Patience. A friend of Flora's named Marcela. She was in her late forties and her kids had gone off to college recently. She was looking for a new chapter in her life. Oliver was already in love with her. Since Trevor liked her and Brodie found nothing bad in her history, it was a good match. "Is everything okay?"

"Yeah. I just promised I'd drop something off before we left."

"Two weeks of sun, sex, and sand sounds incredible," she murmured, leaning her head back against the headrest. She started teaching school in a couple weeks, so Brodie had taken off work so they could spend a couple weeks doing absolutely nothing but relaxing together.

Her summer had ended up very differently than she'd originally planned but she wouldn't have it any other way.

"Oh, I got a call from the detective this morning. Antoine took a deal but he's going away for a solid twelve years at least."

She breathed out a sigh of relief. *Thank God.* She'd known that he was going to jail but at least they were avoiding a stupid trial. And twelve years was a long time with him locked up and unable to hurt anyone. Brodie had also spoken at length with the nanny agency and it turned out that one of the men Antoine had been involved with had harassed them into quitting. They'd been too scared to say anything to anyone. And thankfully Brodie had also figured out how Antoine had gotten into her guest cottage unseen. There had been a couple small holes in the camera security setup around the cottage itself and he'd used those spots to his advantage to sneak in. An outsider wouldn't have been able to make it that far, and everything had since been fixed.

"So, what kind of bathing suits did you pack?" Brodie's grin turned sly as he took another turn.

They were practically living together at this point, with him spending most of his time at her place, mainly because his condo was downtown and was kind of cold. But he hadn't seen anything she'd packed.

She grinned at him. "Who says I packed one at all?"

His fingers tightened around the wheel, his knuckles turning white. "You're determined to kill me, aren't you?"

She simply grinned at him, excited for this adventure. And something told her that this was only the beginning.

"I love you," he murmured, his voice turning serious all of a sudden as he reached out and gently brushed his knuckles over her cheeks.

It wasn't the first time he'd said it, and she didn't get tired of hearing it. She didn't think she ever would. "I love you too."

EPILOGUE

Four months later

"So what's the special occasion?" Patience asked as she sank down onto the quilt Brodie had laid out on the beach. It was way too cold for anyone to be out today, but he'd said he wanted a picnic. Which was kind of nice since Christmas break was coming up and there was no one here right now.

He lifted an eyebrow at her. "Do I need an excuse to take out the woman I love?"

"Good point." She grinned as he pulled out her favorite brand of champagne.

The last few months they'd both been busy with work but he'd officially moved in with her and she loved waking up to him every morning. Well, most mornings, because he did some out-of-town stuff, but they now shared a closet and everything. And his clothes were definitely nicer than hers, considering his custom-made suits. He kept buying her gifts and random things that just made her heart sing with joy. She wasn't used to a man spoiling her and she could admit that she loved it—loved *him* even without the gifts. But she knew it was one of the ways he showed her that he cared.

He pointed the bottle away from them to pop the cork, and once he'd poured their glasses, handed her one.

"Oh, look at that." He pointed to where a plane was doing loops of skywriting.

She laughed as she watched the plane dipping up and down. "Who on earth is out here to even see this?" She froze when she realized that...*they were*. Patience shot him a sideways glance, only to find him watching her with an intense gaze.

Gently, he tipped her chin back up.

She stared at the sky, and with each word that was revealed, her heart rate increased. Holy cannoli.

Will you marry me? was spelled out in giant white clouds.

When she turned to look at him, Brodie was kneeling in front of her, a ring box open. "The last few months with you have been the best of my life. I love you so much it hurts, so much that it surprises me every damn morning that I get to wake up to you. Will you marry me, Patience?"

Tears stung her eyes as she set her glass down. "Yes," she managed to rasp out through her emotion. "Yes!"

Keeping his eyes pinned to hers, he slid the diamond onto her finger.

"You're a very sneaky man," she murmured as he brushed his mouth over hers.

He tugged her into his lap. "I tried to figure out a way to do it with kites, but figured this was just as good since it's at the beach—near where we had our first date. I love you so much, Patience." He captured her mouth with his again before she could answer.

But that was okay. He knew how much she loved him. Soon she was going to get to be Patience MacArthur. And she couldn't wait.

—The End—

ACKNOWLEDGMENTS

In between writing novels and heavier romantic suspense and paranormal romance, novellas give my writer's brain a way to breathe and reset. This is for all my readers who love novellas as much as me. Thank you. I'm also grateful to Kaylea Cross for reading the early version (and as always, asking for more details!), to Julia my wonderful editor, Sarah, for beta reading and Jaycee for another gorgeous cover. Do you get sick of me saying that? I love all your covers!

COMPLETE BOOKLIST

Ancients Rising Series
Ancient Protector
Ancient Enemy
Ancient Enforcer

Darkness Series
Darkness Awakened
Taste of Darkness
Beyond the Darkness
Hunted by Darkness
Into the Darkness
Saved by Darkness
Guardian of Darkness
Sentinel of Darkness
A Very Dragon Christmas
Darkness Rising

Deadly Ops Series
Targeted
Bound to Danger
Chasing Danger (novella)
Shattered Duty
Edge of Danger
A Covert Affair

Endgame Trilogy
Bishop's Knight
Bishop's Queen
Bishop's Endgame

MacArthur Family Series
Falling for Irish
Unintended Target
Saving Sienna

Moon Shifter Series
Alpha Instinct
Lover's Instinct
Primal Possession
Mating Instinct
His Untamed Desire
Avenger's Heat
Hunter Reborn
Protective Instinct
Dark Protector
A Mate for Christmas

O'Connor Family Series
Merry Christmas, Baby
Tease Me, Baby
It's Me Again, Baby
Mistletoe Me, Baby

Red Stone Security Series®
No One to Trust
Danger Next Door
Fatal Deception
Miami, Mistletoe & Murder
Continued...

Red Stone Security Series® continued...
His to Protect
Breaking Her Rules
Protecting His Witness
Sinful Seduction
Under His Protection
Deadly Fallout
Sworn to Protect
Secret Obsession
Love Thy Enemy
Dangerous Protector
Lethal Game
Secret Enemy
Saving Danger

Redemption Harbor Series®
Resurrection
Savage Rising
Dangerous Witness
Innocent Target
Hunting Danger
Covert Games
Chasing Vengeance

Sin City Series (the Serafina)
First Surrender
Sensual Surrender
Sweetest Surrender
Dangerous Surrender
Deadly Surrender

Verona Bay
Dark Memento
Deadly Past

Linked books
Retribution
Tempting Danger

Non-series Romantic Suspense
Running From the Past
Dangerous Secrets
Killer Secrets
Deadly Obsession
Danger in Paradise
His Secret Past

Paranormal Romance
Destined Mate
Protector's Mate
A Jaguar's Kiss
Tempting the Jaguar
Enemy Mine
Heart of the Jaguar

ABOUT THE AUTHOR

Katie Reus is the *New York Times* and *USA Today* bestselling author of the Red Stone Security series, the Darkness series and the Redemption Harbor series. She fell in love with romance at a young age thanks to books she pilfered from her mom's stash. Years later she loves reading romance almost as much as she loves writing it.

However, she didn't always know she wanted to be a writer. After changing majors many times, she finally graduated summa cum laude with a degree in psychology. Not long after that she discovered a new love. Writing. She now spends her days writing dark paranormal romance and sexy romantic suspense.

For more information on Katie please visit her website: www.katiereus.com.

Made in the USA
Coppell, TX
14 March 2021